FIRE SPEEDS THE WILD PONY

Robert Stewart

ISBN: 978-1-8381272-5-1 (paperback)
ISBN: 978-1-8381272-6-8 (ebook)

The Moors

His breathing bellowed inside his rib cage and broke in a hot mist on the moorland air. Other sounds toyed with the general quiet. One came from an unusual-looking bird. In time, the horse had got to know most of the wildlife that nested in the thick scrub. This bird was different. It had a gently arched head that sank into the bursting breath of its body. More distinctively, its bottom half was completely white, which contrasted with its rusty brown plumage. It almost looked like a ball dipped in whitewash. It stood on top of a large boulder, the faintest breeze ruffling its feathers, staring at the horse. Then it flew off.

The horse watched it pitch weightlessly into the air and set an erratic course along the ridge. With no obvious intention, he gave chase.

The bird bobbed unsurely, evading the attraction

of forces all around it. It would rise and fall with the shape of the terrain, at times sinking low enough to almost disappear with the lurking butterworts and other bog plants. All the same, it never wavered in its chosen path. It had more puff than the horse had imagined; it kept going and going, beating a path with a small pulse of determination.

The ridge climbed gradually but unevenly, rising to the crest of small hillocks then descending through waterlogged peat from where it rediscovered an upwards course. The sky was a grey wash to complement the boisterous pride of the bird's belly, and blew a blustery blast over the vast and mostly featureless open spaces of the upland moors. The bird, it seemed, was making for the highest point, a place so exposed that it repelled most creatures. The horse was exhilarated by the chase, by the mystery of the bird's purpose (if it had one).

The final ascent was made more difficult by the mulchy mess in which the recent rainfall had left the hillside. The mud and tangled heather clutched at his hooves and pulled him down. The wind made the hillside shiver.

He slowed to a gentle trot as he reached the plateau. The summit was the rough shape of an expanded circle, strewn with smoothed and steady rocks and stones, and the occasional ungainly obtrusion of red sandstone.

On the far side of the summit, he would meet an escarpment. This led the way down to a plain, disturbed only by passing ripples in a journey out to the horizon. Behind him the ridge marked the way of his ascent and carved out an eruption of land between the plain, and a verdant valley on the other side of the ridge.

He came to a halt. The air was chill. The steady breeze, which had been checked by the shelter of the hills, had become a biting wind.

But he couldn't see the bird.

Instead, he saw something else; it was in the distance, down on the plain. Against the haze, it was not always easy to make out and it would disappear and reappear in only a moment, as if the wind kept knocking it down each time it stood up.

The horse walked a little closer, so that he approached the edge of the summit and stood before a sharp descent. He had never seen a light like this before; he had seen some lights twinkling at night in the basin of the valley, or lonely torches down on the plain. Whatever it was, its pulse was stronger than any other torch he had seen, but more unstable. Which made him wonder what it could be – what had caused it? Or was it not the sort of thing that had a cause? Was it an unknown creature? Or was it the outward sign of some event?

The light held an uncanny appeal, offering just enough of itself to keep his attention without disclosing its true nature. Then, of course, there was the unusual bird; two unusual things, one of which had led him to the other. To his mind, they hailed from the same place. And if the bird had led him to the light, why had it done so? Was it a sign to which he was meant to respond? Or was he reading into the events more than he should? He couldn't know.

That's enough, now. Leave it there.

So came his familiar thoughts. Something was toying with his curiosity, and, in a predictable fashion shaped by long hours and days of foraging and roaming, speculations gathered towards a groundswell of expectation. He knew, of course, that he would have to check the musings of his mind and let the scratchy limbs of the shrub bring him back to familiar terrain. Yet for all the reservations of good sense, he wanted to indulge the appearance of signs and their obscure meaning. As always, they appealed to that part of him that had always want to break out.

There's no harm in finding out just a little more.

One way he might do that was simple: he could ask some of the other horses on the hillside.

He made his way down the ridge, walking slowly. Further along, where the moorland rose over the cob of a hill, he could see one of the packs picking their way. He set out in their direction.

The summit from which he had descended bulged out from the main line of the ridge, and a small path ran at an angle along the lee side of the hill down towards the green pastures and meandering streams of the valley. The path was well known, and the horses would often follow it through the folds of overgrown bracken to lower slopes. It wandered eventually into a copse of trees growing in the shadow of a rocky outcrop. On hot days, the horses would sometimes descend into the shade and drink from the small stream that trickled down from the moorland.

The path had been made by a community of men who lived in the valley below. They spent their days in a large building. Few other people had settled there, except for those who, in one way or another, had a connection to them.

The horse, or for that matter any other creatures on the hillside, knew very little about the men, except that they were there, and in their own quiet way, they tended to the land around. Every now and then, this brought them out in ones or twos, though never in large groups. Most of the horses on the moorland were untroubled by the men and paid little attention to them, but the horse saw them in the same way he saw anything else outlying the ordinary – with curiosity and keenness.

It was assumed that the men had trodden out the path up the hillside, not least because it clearly led to their home on the valley floor. And yet the men were almost never seen on the ridges and moorland. Which is why the sight of a man from the community climbing up the path counted as another unusual event.

The horse knew the man came from the valley, not only because he was climbing from that direction, but because all the men in the community wore the same clothes: a black robe with a hood. Sometimes they wore the hood up, at other times down. This figure, presumably to protect himself from the elements, wore the hood up, so that the horse could only see the shape of the figure and a shadow across his face.

The horse stopped, a little way from the point at which the path met the ridge. The man moved slowly but lightly. It was difficult to know when the man saw the horse, because his hood veiled his eyes. The nearer the man came, the more his chin and its wisps of grey hair dared to find a place in the light.

The worn path gave way to grass as it reached the ridge. The man shuffled forward and, appearing to look at the ground, he turned his head so that he was looking directly at the horse. Face-to-face, the horse could just make out the man's features – he was thin, almost shockingly so. His skin hugged his jaw and cheekbones, and his eyes, still cast in darkness, receded into their sockets.

The figure might have looked menacing, but the horse could detect no ill-will. The horse wanted to approach and was about to make the first move when the man withdrew his arms from his robe to remove his hood.

Hair like a light scattering of snow clung to his face, and the sockets of his eyes were so sunk that they had left the glistening blue orbs at their centre over-exposed. A thin rash of hair grew about the man's head. His appearance was weather-worn, leathered and harsh.

Again, the horse started to approach, but the man turned his attention elsewhere. Leaving his hood down, he continued his steady shuffle forward, until he found a place at the peak of the ridge. From there, he looked out onto the plain.

The horse watched the man, and watched the man watching the light. A new part of the wider event they were witnessing became apparent. First the bird, then the light, now the man – they were all connected.

At last, the horse moved. He walked forward slowly, lowering his head a little, to follow the footsteps of the robed figure. The horse exhaled and thrust his nose under the man's, seeking any attention that might meet his curiosity. The man smiled at the horse, reached up with his right arm and patted the horse about the nose; the man hooked his left arm under the horse's head, so that the two of them were lightly locked together. In this embrace, the man looked out on the plain once more. A breeze ruffled their hair; there was enough cold in the air to expose their breath.

The man said something, his gaze still fixed on the beacon.

*

'Why do you want to know?' asked Sweetbriar.

'I just thought you might have heard – I thought one of you might have heard something.'

'About a light on the plain?'

'It's quite unusual,' said the horse. 'I have never seen anything like it before.'

'But why do you want to know? What does it matter? So what if there's a light on the horizon? I don't think anyone else cares very much.'

'Perhaps they haven't seen it? Though it's plain enough to see.'

Sweetbriar belonged to one of the small herds that roamed around the moorland. They usually lived on or about the ridge but strayed to different places. The horse had spoken with her many times; she was the only member of the herd he had come to know.

'No-one knows anything,' she replied, not paying the horse's questions much mind.

'One of the brothers – he came up just now. Did you see? They hardly ever take the trouble to come up here.'

'No, I didn't see. I haven't seen any of them for longer than I can remember. What they do is their affair.'

'It can't be a coincidence.'

'What can't?'

'The light and the brother.'

'You think …?'

'And there was a bird.'

'There are many birds.'

'This one was different.'

Sweetbriar sighed.

'You should let it go. Nothing good will come of it. Besides, I can't see the coinci … what interest would the brother have in the light? And what's more it's none of our business.'

'Something tells me …'

'Yes …?'

The other horses in the herd were beginning to drift over the moorland. Sweetbriar wanted to follow.

'Something tells me that it is our business.'

'*Our* business? Or *your* business?' she asked with a

smile.

'I … I didn't …'

'We have a place here; all of us. We know this place and belong to it. It's dangerous to stray. Running here, running there, chasing every unusual sound or happening. You are restless and you always have been. I don't believe you will ever be truly satisfied – something stirs you. The others said when you were a young foal that no good would come of it. You would do well to ignore all these 'strange' occurrences. But you won't. You won't.'

The horse recognised the truth in Sweetbriar's words. It wasn't the first time they had held this sort of conversation. He had rarely, if ever, stayed too close to the company of a herd because he found them too set in their ways. The life and events around him had always fired his interest. A grouse, a lost hare, the furtive movements of a snake – whatever it was, it would always capture his imagination, and whenever his interest was roused, he found it hard not to follow, or let it lead him on. He was always straying, charging across the heather, looking for something. Even sounds, strange fell cries, garbled songs carried on the wind, or the faintest tintinnabulation, could work him into a delirium, and he would chase the noise all about the hills, until its echo was lost in the distance of the valley.

Besides, he was different; they had told him so many times. His character was merely the close ally of his appearance – the other packs strayed about the hills in packs and clearly all belonged to the same breed; but they had made it clear that he didn't look like them. He was stronger, sleeker, as smooth and streamlined as sedimentary rock fashioned by the aeons. Which, for a time at least, had begged the questions: why and where had he come from? None of them knew the answers, and so he had come to accept his place as an exception, even if he was not reconciled to the staid life the other horses chose.

Sweetbriar was right; something in him would not rest.

And even looking for the validation she would not give him, he could feel his irritation stir. Why, he wanted to ask, was she so content to drift about the hills, passively accepting the murmurings of life that reached them? Was she not at least a little curious? Whatever it was in his nature that set him apart from the other horses, he was sure – he would even say that he knew it – that it came via an instinct bred into his bones through a different form of life, or a different way of living. Here, he was an outsider, but elsewhere he felt sure that he might find the answer to the riddle of his inclination.

'I don't know why you come to us with these questions. You know we don't have the answers. But then you know what I think.'

'What do you mean?'

'I think you know what answer you want to hear.'

Sweetbriar turned to follow the others.

*

Darkness drew out the light on the horizon. When the horse had seen it for the first time, it had looked like a flash. In the dark, it flickered with intemperate rage.

The sky was clear, and the moon was bright enough to mark out the curvature of the hills. Only a gentle breeze ruffled the bristles of heather. The horse stood on the ridge, looking out on the plain. They were right, of course. He had known they were right when they said it. Other horses – other creatures – would mind their own business, but he was drawn to the light, as he was drawn to all odd intrusions, noises, and events.

From this thought, two others followed: in the first the vast emptiness and silence of the hills fired his curiosity, as though the sheer scale of his loneliness made the appearance of anything more real; in the second, he thought he simply had to leave the moorland and see such lights for what they were.

A whorl of wind circled up the ridge. It startled him. A spirit was out walking. It was nearby. Sure enough, as he tilted his head just a little to the right, he could make out the grey-white edges of a figure shimmering through the gorse on the common. The horse knew not to hope for much from a spirit, but he approached it all the same, taking a slow and steady trot, timed to meet the figure's ascent.

It was hard to know what the spirit had once been: a human or another animal, maybe even another horse (even if his intuition told him otherwise). Its shape, the outline of which suggested the last vestiges of life, dissembled, and disappeared with each forward thrust of movement. The horse did not call or disturb the spirit, except by making his presence known. The spirit offered no signal either, but the horse knew he was in its field of awareness because its steady but sure forward trudge came to a halt.

'You are a horse,' said the spirit eventually. 'Where did you come from? Did you flee?'

'I live here, in the hills,' said the horse.

The horse drew on the night air and took time to weigh up his companion.

'Where did you come from?' asked the horse.

'Away, down there,' said the spirit.

Its voice, like its form, failed as it spoke, as if its

whole being were departing and soon there would be nothing left.

'On the plain?' asked the horse.

'That's right. Down there,' said the spirit.

Now the horse thought he had some measure of the spirit.

'You were coming up the hillside in a hurry. Why? What's your hurry?'

'To get away. It's lost. Now is the time to run.'

As the spirit spoke, the horse could just make out an eye, a bead of hazel-green no longer tethered to a source of life. Like everything else about the spirit, it was fading. He could also see part of a jaw, badly fractured and mutilated. A human, then? But even with the hideous and cryptic remnant of fleshly features, the spirit might have been an animal – a large dog, perhaps.

'Where are you going?' asked the horse.

'I don't know.'

'You are dead,' said the horse. 'You are killed, I think.'

'I want to get away,' said the spirit.

The horse looked back over the plain, to the light.

'Something is burning,' he said. 'Down there on the plain, something is burning.'

'Yes,' said the spirit.

'What is it?'

'The tower. And the chapel. They may fall. Before

long, they may fall.'

'You've seen the flame?'

'I have seen it.'

'What is it?'

'A great fire.'

'Where did it come from?'

'I must keep going. It's late. I must get away.'

The horse shuffled impatiently.

'Where are you going? You are dead.'

'I must keep going.'

The horse thought that the spirit didn't know its own mind. Even its words were the last fragments of an intention no longer decisively guided.

'There is a place on the far side of the hill.'

Insofar as the spirit could make any clear movements, it turned to look the horse squarely in the face. The horse was surprised and even more surprised by the words that followed.

'I have spoken with many horses,' said the spirit. 'You are a good horse, and gatekeeper to my destination. I see you, though you might not know it. I see your mind, how it is cast and inclined. We cross paths, each favouring the opposite direction. Why do you want to go down there? Are you clear about what you expect to find?

For who gives in and turns his eye

Back to darkness from the sky,
Loses while he looks below
All that up with him may go."

'What do you mean?' asked the horse, startled by the sudden change of tone.

The spirit's eyeball rolled, so that its features melted into disfigured formlessness and drifted into the night. The horse could see at once that he would get no more – there was no more to be had.

'I must keep going,' it said in the same ethereal voice. 'I must get away.'

It started to move forward in its shimmering shuffle, wisps of its presence steaming into the night. The same unguided intention kept whatever remained of it anchored to the earth, but it would not last long.

The horse watched it glide over the moorland, becoming harder and harder to make out, until either it was too distant to see, or there was nothing left of it to be seen. His eyes lingered, then he turned his head to stare at the flame bellowing in the dark night.

*

The events of the last few days troubled the horse – they seemed to signal some sort of imbalance or intrusion into their otherwise still and undisturbed world. Where was the bird leading him? Why had the robed man climbed up onto the ridge? From where and what had the spirit fled? And what was the light on the horizon?

These questions weighed on him, so that the events and his restive mind unsettled him right to the core. A part of him believed – or wanted to believe – that they were all connected; and that each question, in some sense, had the same answer. But he couldn't be sure. Another part of him thought that he shouldn't over-react. All of these recent events were certainly unusual, but he also had no reason to think that they wouldn't settle down, and that the world – his world – would return to normal in time.

Most other animals on the moorland, including the other horses, reacted this way, insofar as they reacted at all. Another part of him, a part that he couldn't keep under control, saw the last few days as an invitation, or signs that pointed beyond the simple life on the hillside he had always lived. They inflamed the spark of curiosity that set him apart from the other horses and made him wonder about life on the plain. And if these were signs, what did they signify? Why had they all occurred within a short space of time? Were they a call? Was someone or something calling to him?

He had no way to know how he might answer any

of these questions, but he knew that if something was calling him, he shouldn't ignore it. To do nothing, to pretend that nothing had changed in the hope that it would all go away, was blinkered.

Then how should he answer the call? What should he do? The answer was obvious, and the excitement bristled on his back. He would walk down one of the tracks on the hillside. From there, he would keep walking out onto the plain, guided by the fire on the horizon.

He had thought about leaving the hillside before; there were many routes down into one of the valleys that looked like they led into lower lands. The plain was the most immediate and obvious enticement, and its visible contrast with the world he knew, was the readiest supply of kindle for his imagination. He had looked out on the plain many times, trying to discern things that were more alive than the patchwork of fields and common land. He felt sure that other creatures eked out some sort of existence there, but the manner and character of their living he could only surmise – and what he didn't know only made him more curious.

Although he might have thought about leaving the hills before, he had never had a real reason and he had no way to make sense of what he might expect. It was, he had thought, like trying to imagine life as a star in the night sky. And yet his energy and independence of mind told him that he could not settle for life on the high moorland forever. His was a spirit in search of more than exercise; he was looking for something, or rather it felt to him that the impulses of his body were looking for a shape and direction they would never really find in the hills, no matter how often he gave free reign to his body in maniacal gallops and voracious discovery.

Every instinct told him that there was more to the world than his hills, and that the spright and vigour in his body would respond to ways of living he had not yet experienced.

I should go. Now is the time to go.

These words resounded in his mind, repeating and echoing, to the point that they became a spur to movement. He moved closer to the plain without taking his eyes off the light. He wanted to see it; he wanted to see the burning tower for himself.

If it is calling to me, I should answer.

*

The same bird came to him in the same place. As before, it perched on the boulder. Where it had come from and when it had appeared, the horse couldn't say. He looked up and it was there. The breeze ruffled its feathers. It stared at him before it flew off.

The horse hesitated, as he watched the creature flutter away over the moorland, but he couldn't contain his excitement, and before the bird was blown from view, he set out in pursuit.

This time they took a different direction – the bird flew along the opposite line of the ridge, but with the same unsteady command of the air. The wind blew it one way, then another. The horse managed to keep up with it, but the precarious nature of its flight made it harder to follow. Several times it seemed to have disappeared completely, and the horse had to halt his movement and scan his surroundings before it popped up from somewhere and the chase resumed.

The destination of the bird's journey was, if anything, even less clear than before. This way along the ridge didn't lead to an obvious place; there were many different routes, all leading to different places. And this time the bird wanted to go much further. He followed the ridge on a gentle descent before it climbed up onto the sprawling heathland. From experience, the horse knew this area was disorienting; you might set out in one direction and find yourself somewhere else entirely. Something about the featureless moorland made it easy to get lost.

The bird was untroubled. It flew over the heather with no sign of hesitation or disorientation. It kept up a straight line of flight until the land took a sudden descent onto a grassy common. From there and apparently with no loss of stamina, it picked out a swift and decisive route over the grasses, until they came to an underused track looping around the bloated contour of the hill. Still the bird kept going.

The horse's curiosity and keenness to keep pace only increased the longer their shared journey continued. He half-expected the bird to just disappear into a bush, or come to rest on a branch, from where it would glance at the horse, as if to say, *Why have you been following me, you stupid horse?!*

Except the bird didn't stop. It found its way to a spot the horse couldn't remember. He had explored most parts of the hills, but tended to remain high up on the moorland. Most of the journey they had taken so far, he had recognised, but this lower track was less familiar and the dwindling path it became had no place in his memory.

A narrow pass crept up on them, squeezing the two creatures into a confined corridor between the grassy slopes. This short passage, though the horse was hardly aware of it at the time, had something unnatural about it – the air was inhospitable to life; it became more rarefied the further they went. With it, all noise faded away. The horse couldn't even detect the sound of his own hooves. The steady beat of his mind remained, even if he harboured few thoughts at the time. His head, of all things, made the most noise in the confined space of the passage. His brain was somehow resilient enough to survive where all other senses had quickly fallen away; but even his mind was under assault, withering or fading as he moved through the close air and in touching distance of the mudstone wall. He could still see the bird fluttering ahead, but the pass erased everything else, as if drawing attention to their journey by abstracting it, until only the bird would remain and finally vanish into oblivion.

Then, in a moment, they emerged from the pass onto a part of the hills the horse had never seen before. His sense of the world wasn't exactly restored, but sounds came back to him and he could feel the chill wind broach his body. The place was unusually quiet – even for the hills.

The bird had led them out of the contracted pass

into view of a small lake overshadowed by a looming and precipitous bluff. The dark rise of the hills made them look bitten by cold and forgotten by time. A small switchback path wound down from their position at the end of the pass towards the water. The bird, unconcerned by the need for this sort of way-marking, simply flew straight ahead.

The horse, partly arrested by the novelty of the scene, was slow to keep up, and his need to follow the path meant that he gained distance from the bird. Making his way down the path as fast as he could, he arrived at the water to find that he had lost sight of the bird. He cast about in all directions, searching one way then another. He manoeuvred around on all fours to retrace the route he had taken, hoping he might glimpse a flash of tail and feathers. He only saw the creature once he turned again to consider the lake. It hopped out of nowhere to land on a large slab of rock protruding over the water's edge. The bird looked at the horse. The horse took a step forward and then the bird launched out in a straight line of flight. The horse watched it glide.

He rushed up to the edge of the lake. With the thought that he might somehow swim it, he glanced down. He saw the face of a horse disturbed and disrupted by the unsettled temper of the water's surface. The horse was shocked and not a little startled, but at first glance he was somehow hooked by the sight of it. He peered closer, hoping that the nearer he got, the more he might be able to wrestle the image into a state of stillness.

Then the horse in the water spoke.

'Where are you going, horse?' it said.

'Who, me?'

'Yes, where are you going? What are you doing?'

The horse didn't know how to understand what was happening.

'There was a bird,' he explained. 'I followed it here.'

'A bird?'

'Yes.'

'And it brought you here?'

'Yes.'

'Was it a white bird?'

'Do you know it?'

'I have seen it before. Why did it bring you here?'

'I don't know.'

'Then why did you follow it?'

'I followed it before.'

'And where did it lead you before?'

'High up into the hills – onto a summit.'

'What did you find there?'

'I saw a light.'

'A light?'

'I saw a light down on the plain.'

The horse in the water thought for a second.

'Did you see this light?'

The horse in the water disappeared and an image of the light he had seen on the plain took its place. The horse peered closer into the water.

'Yes,' he said quietly. 'Yes, that was the light I saw.'

'I thought as much,' replied the voice of the horse in the water.

'What is it?' asked the horse.

'What's what?'

'The light – what's the light?'

The horse waited as the water let go of all the images. Somehow the horse knew that something else was stirring, and then he saw a storm of men on horses riding through a gate. Smoke and cries stood about them. A boy ran towards the scene, but one of the riders thrust his sword at the boy, driving it straight through his eye socket. The horse's head shook at the sight of it.

Then the scene vanished and in its place he saw a cloth with the embroidered image of a horse floating freely before him. Human hands appeared around its edges. They belonged to a young girl, who gripped the cloth, as she danced about a meadow, skipping and spinning. She was singing something, but the horse couldn't see or hear what exactly. Then, as quickly as she had appeared, she faded from view.

The meadow changed. The long grasses and flowers withered into the ground and became a dried field of old stones. Light had been sucked out of the scene, and a small fire flickered by an old ash tree. A rope was draped over one of its branches and an upturned bucket stood adjacent to the fire.

'He is here,' whispered a voice quietly. But it wasn't the voice of the horse in the water. It sounded more like the voice of a woman. 'He has been waiting for you.'

A thin breeze caused the rope tied to the branch of the tree to move. He thought he could feel the air shift about his haunches, then a laugh, blackened with bad business, rasped in his other ear and he felt a sharp and sudden stab of pain in his left side.

The horse whinnied, withdrew from the water and turned to see what was about him. Nothing was about him. No-one had crept up on him. This unusual spot in the hills was as empty as when he had first arrived.

The horse looked back at the water. All the visions had gone, leaving only the ripple brought by the breeze. Looking over the lake to the far side, he met the foot of the cliff. He thought he might catch sight of the bird staring back at him, beckoning him towards other secrets. But there was nothing; he was the only creature in this lonely place.

Not knowing quite what to do, he drifted back towards the water. He looked down at it again, expecting to catch sight of more scenes and to hear more voices. He leaned forward to break its surface with his nose, but this conjured no more trickery to life. Finally, with no real reason and not to quench any thirst, he took a drink. He held the water in his mouth, as he thought about the things he had just seen and heard. Then he swallowed.

The horse traced the water's edge a little way towards the escarpment, unable to let go of his fascination with the phantasms. After who knows how long, he drifted away from the water slowly and thoughtlessly, climbing over some ground sparsely patched with rough grass. This paved the way towards a lightly trodden path that climbed up behind the cliff. The horse ambled upwards untethered to the slow movements and volition of his body.

The way, broken by boggy peat and sudden bursts of overgrowth, led all the way to the top of the cliff. Obscured by the same daze, he found that he was, again, high up in the hills.

In taking in his whereabouts, he thought he recognised some of the hills as places he had seen, albeit from different locations and at different angles; but he was sure that he had never been to this place before.

The wind was more forceful at the top of the cliff. His coat tried to take leave from his body. He wasn't thinking clearly. Something had clouded his mind, leaving him in this deadened state. Even so, he had never felt quite so calm, so willing to yield the strains of his life. In this frame of mind, he absorbed the things he had seen; he could sense them, as if they were still about him, which made him a little frightened. If he were to drop his guard, they might suddenly assault him or injure him. But he also thought he knew that there was nothing to fear – really, they were just visions and nothing more.

One way he conceived in the moment to test the tension between these two thoughts, was to drop his vigilance altogether, to feel the spectre of each image near him and know they could do him no harm. The horse looked out over the hills, down at the lake, and finally, he closed his eyes. Surrendering to the darkness, he waited. Slowly, his fears receded. Only the calmness remained.

In this state, he lost all sense of time. Indeed, he could see, when eventually he snapped out of this reverie, that the day was coming to its close. The familiar and hungry beat of his body slowed down, in a way that was not dissimilar to falling asleep. He was still aware of it, of its rhythms and pulses, but they had become smaller, more insignificant. Quietness gathered all about him, and the usual noise that made him restless, and the flow of thoughts and speculations that taunted him, deferred to this quietude, and were subsumed under it.

When, at last, he started to move, his body felt new – or that the act of movement renewed it, again much as he might feel upon waking and shaking his limbs into their first contortions of the day. Except this experience questioned his body and all the restless meanings and attachments that came with it.

As he found more life and trudged with more speed back to his familiar haunts near the ridge, in sight of the mysterious beacon that had caused him so much concern, he was moved to think about what had just happened. He didn't rightly know how to make sense of it. Was everything not what he had, at first, imagined? He was even tempted to think that the unusual visions and the chastening spell they had cast on him, were a kind of warning – and that they came from the hills, almost as if they spoke for them, qualifying and checking the temptations he had entertained and which had, until the day before, fixed his will on a course of action that might change his life. If the light was calling to him, was this another voice whose meaning he was meant to understand?

The three images he had seen in the water and the strange sensation of pain that had brought them to a close, had amounted to nothing. They were phantoms, a trick played in the cold ripples of the tarn. Was this how he was meant to understand all the thoughts he had begun to entertain? Were the images he had seen intimations of a life on the plain that, understood in its proper light, was a shadow, a vacant spirit expending its last breath before it disappeared?

He walked, alone and dispirited, over the heather. No birds tried to catch his attention. No other signs or strange events tried to make themselves known.

I should stay here, then, I suppose.

He didn't resent his life on the moors. It was their serenity and great silence that made him think again. As he reached the ridge at the edge of the mountains, he found himself settling on a new conclusion. If the light on the horizon was a call, he would lose something in heeding it, and there seemed some reason to think anything he might gain would vanish like the images in the tarn.

I should stay here.

*

Days followed in which the absence of any further aberrant happenings and the tentative resumption of normal life helped to cool and quash the thoughts of adventure that the horse had started to entertain.

No, Sweetbriar is right. It is best not to stray.

After a day, he was reconciled to his decision and even some of the quickness that had stoked his blood, began to abate. Instead, the hillside conveyed him in a thoughtless drift, and where his mind had met any object with a thirst for conquest, now it wandered freely.

For all the thrill of pursuing the bird and tracing each departure from the mean back to a cause, he felt calmer, more content, and despite what the other horses said about him, more himself. The instinct to pursue his delirious interests was matched by a more sober instinct to let them go. By the second day after his visit to the tarn, he started to follow a route away from the ridge, almost as if he had exhausted his curiosity about the plain and was prepared to wholeheartedly embrace the thin atmosphere of the central mountain range.

He took a long traverse over a high hunchback of moors, descending briefly to skirt the edge of woodland that canopied the entirety of another valley he could see arching off to his left. From there, he climbed up onto a vantage point from where he could reckon a panoramic view of the range. The hills were interminable or appeared that way.

The third day he spent entirely alone. The heather, by a change of geology, didn't grow in the same way, and shake holes pockmarked the terrain. He could hear no birds, see no other horses, and find little sign of life in any form. The hills drew him closer to their kernel of silence, and he carried on in the same ambling sojourn for much of the night.

*

When dawn came, it was clear something had happened. Ordinarily, the hillside and the smattering of life that populated it, were free and untroubled. Not this day. Every creature was in a state of disturbance, though almost none of them knew its cause. The birds chattered restlessly, and the creatures of the earth stayed put.

The horse went on a search at once, not knowing where to look or for what. He sensed his way in an aimless and meandering fashion. No-one knew what had happened, except that something was not right. He met one other horse, who said and knew very little but looked frightened. Before too long, his instinct led him back in the direction of the ridge. As he neared the familiar valley and caught sight of the elaborate buildings the men called their home, a gentle breeze swept over him. The air was usually clean, but as it gusted by, he caught a smell, one that made his head thunder.

The mephitic odour became more powerful the closer he came to it. He had come down from the ridge onto another grassy common. The source of the smell was hidden behind a sudden lurch towards the valley. The first thing he saw was the eyes of a dead horse staring lifelessly at him. That sight alone made him stop. The eyes brought him into their deathly domain; the flickering fable of the creature's being had gone and to see it was murderous, like staring his own mortality in the face.

Then he saw the rest of the horse. It had been savaged – the remains of its stomach had been ripped wide open and its rib cage was exposed to the open air; its legs fell at broken and contorted angles.

He had never seen a creature so brutally assaulted. It took him a long time before he could muster the wherewithal to move. What sort of creature would have the strength to do this to a horse? A bear perhaps? A pack of wolves? The way the poor creature had been destroyed was almost too senseless to suit the character of a predator – of any kind.

The horse approached the rotting body carefully, tilting his head, first one side then the other, to study the assault from different angles. Then, as the full range of his awareness returned to him, he noticed how quiet it was roundabout. No birds were singing, no creatures haunted the grassy slopes, even from a distance – somehow, they all knew to stay away. Which made him uneasy. Were they right to stay away? He glanced at the dead horse warily, gave a plaintive whinny, and started to retreat.

He turned to retrace his steps, when he caught the sight of some other creature above him, looking down from the hillside at the scene. It was a man, and unless he was mistaken, it was the same figure he had seen before. The horse whinnied again and stopped, not sure what to make of it. The man stood quite still. His hood covered his head, shrouding his face so that it was hard to see where he was looking.

Before long, the man turned his head only a small fraction, but enough to suggest his gaze had moved to face the horse. The man lowered his hood. The horse saw that the man's expression was grave, stretched, and forlorn. Then he took a step forward.

The horse startled. Alive to the anguish he could see before him, the man withdrew his foot and without taking his eyes from the horse, slowly took a seat cross-legged on the ground. There, he waited. For a time, the man watched the horse. Then, once he was reassured that the horse was a little calmer, he brought his attention back to the corpse. Across the short distance between them, the horse could hear the man muttering some words under his breath.

Man and horse stayed in these positions, letting whatever skittish emotions were in the air settle. Finally, the horse trotted slowly up the hillside, skirting around the steep drop, from where the man meditated on the scene of carnage. When he reached the same part of the hillside, he expected a reaction, but the man's face was fixed – or appeared to be – on the disfigured body of the dead horse. The same mutterings came from his mouth.

Coming a little closer, the horse was surprised to see that the man's eyes were closed. The horse trod forward quietly, leaned towards the man's face, and nuzzled him gently with his nose so that he might solicit the interest of the robed figure's veiled eyes. The two creatures studied the opaque pulse of character and intelligence to which they each bore witness.

*

The dead horse stayed with him, ghosting his movements for the rest of the day and into the night. At times he felt the spirit of the creature was near at hand, and he found it necessary to glance behind him, half-expecting to see its spectral outline on his tail.

Except he knew that the horse's spirit had long since departed, and his intuition was just the fever of his own mind, stirred up by the horror of what he had witnessed. Like everything else he had seen in recent days, he wanted to make sense of it. Except, he thought, perhaps it made no sense. What if it was just a fleeting moment of senseless violence or cruelty? True, that would be unusual – in his experience exceptional – for the life he and the other horses had known. Then again, that didn't make it impossible.

All the same, he couldn't resist an alternative way of thinking about the murder. Something had caused a disturbance out on the plain, and all the unusual things he had seen were effects, or secondary consequences of it. Whatever had killed the horse, even if it was only proximate, had some connection to the light on the horizon. It was as if someone had felled a patch of woodland, and in doing so displaced all manner of creatures that would have otherwise remained where they were.

Still, the cautionary refrain at the back of his mind told him that he would be sensible to take refuge in the places he knew well and stick closer to one of the packs until things settled down. The signs he had seen, as the most recent one made clear, were signs of danger, not promise or hope. Should he respond to them, he would be making a pact with the danger, ceding the better part of him for something double-dealing and quick.

And furthermore, what if these weren't signs at all, at least not signs that held any meaning for him? Something was happening. That much was evident. That didn't mean it was calling to him. The sense of a calling could have just been a figment born of the years he had spent wandering in the hills, imagining and dreaming of something beyond them.

The dead horse haunted him in another way, a deeper way. He felt a kinship with it, not only because they belonged to the same species, but because its death spoke to his circumstances. In a certain sense, he thought that he was the dead horse. The picture of carnage was a peculiar kind of reflection, one that nature in its subtle arrangements could produce from time to time; it revealed a picture of what he would become and a warning of what, without acting on his natural impulses, he already was. It was this thought that returned as he strolled aimlessly over the moors.

That night the hillside was even quieter than usual. There was almost no wind, and the presence of nocturnal animals went undetected. Nothing stirred and no strange occurrences, further signs or mysterious calls came to answer the questions in his mind. Only the light on the horizon remained. In the clearness of the night, the horse thought it had grown larger and brighter. The silence seemed to point back to the light; each preceding event had borne its strange message, and now vacated the air so that the horse might consider the one lasting mystery. The light was inviting him, reaching out to him through the darkness. He could feel the distant glow on the bulb of his eyes.

*

The horse waited for the sun to rise before he set out across the heather. He didn't pay much mind to the creatures about him, not that they showed much interest. A few birds erupted from the undergrowth in short puffs of energy, and grouse warbled at the sound of his hooves. The moorland fell to a path; a few strides along led to a switch-back turn that opened the way for the track, cutting a route across the hillside. The horse stopped; his head lowered to assess the way. He looked out onto the plain, where, even by the fresh glare of the morning, he could see the light in the distance.

The movement of a creature caught his attention. It was the same unusual bird. He was certain it was the same bird because it had the same markings. As before, it had settled on a small outcrop of stone, where it waited patiently. The horse expected it to flutter off again, but it stayed anchored to its temporary perch.

The horse tried to guess the bird's mind. He looked around, thinking he might find another creature or a sign he was intended to interpret. There was nothing. Was this a warning? Or the opposite? Was the bird imploring him not to descend from his altitude? Or was it urging him on? The horse looked down the track once more, then back at the bird, hoping it might react or indicate what the horse should do. The bird was unflinching. Coming to the realisation that he could expect nothing from it, the horse looked again at the way ahead.

He set off down the track.

40

Fire Speeds the Wild Pony

The Plain

He built up speed, his trot gradually taking the form of a canter. The track, after a short while, lurched over an undulation and swept around the crescent of the ridge. There it descended more steeply and a short way ahead he could see the path disappear into woodland. The shade from the trees made the path appear to vanish into half-light, which meant he didn't see the man walking out of the woodland until they were almost upon each other. He had found some pace by this point, and he was so startled by the appearance of a human that he exclaimed at a high pitch. The man was disordered but not panicked or threatened. He raised his arms to calm the horse and shuffled sideways.

The horse retreated to the edge of the woodland. Noises came from behind him. The man was speaking; he made similar gestures to placate and console the horse's distress. The sudden collision with so many emotions meant that the horse didn't have time to think. Surprise, panic, fear and a little fight were all only just starting to subside. The horse gave an involuntary dance on the spot, from where he began to take the measure of the man. Was it the same robed individual he had seen on the hillside? He thought it was unlikely that it would be anyone else. If the figure was the robed man he had already met twice before – or even one of his kind – then his instinct was to trust him.

The horse settled his breathing and waited for his movements to follow. This gave him the chance to examine the man a little more closely. He looked ever-so-slightly different. For one thing, though it meant very little to the horse, he wore different clothes. The black robe had gone. More noticeably for the horse, this man gave him a different feeling. The robed figure he had met on the hillside was calm, self-possessed and unfazed by the presence of wild animals. This man was more tense. He moved gingerly, eager to win a measure of trust; but beneath the surface, conflict was at work in him.

The horse could see no reason not to trust the man. He was not dangerous. The horse was sure about that; and he was just as sure that the man meant well. In these brief moments, the man and the horse stepped cautiously towards a state of mutual trust. Something about the way each behaved to the other, once they had overcome the initial panic, suggested a concealed purpose. The man wanted something. The horse could see it clearly.

Then it occurred to the horse: if the light on the horizon had been calling to him, and he expected his descent from the hills to be met with a reply – was this it? Would the man lead him towards the light? He wasn't sure and he didn't know how to understand it all.

Sniffing the air between them, the horse moved closer to his newest companion.

*

The man was a farmer. He tended a wide acreage in the shadow of the hills and could scarcely contain something like delight as they walked down the hillside. He expected the horse to protest or run off at any moment and couldn't quite believe how easily he managed to guide the horse through the gate of the farm and into the stables.

That night the farmer supplied food, then spent some time watching the horse, patting and rubbing him. He bobbed in and out of the stable to study, even admire, his new prize.

Before the light went out of the day altogether, the farmer brought into the stable two other horses. Both were startled to meet their new company; they strained at their halters. The farmer walked from the stable, withholding a smile. The three horses waited as night squeezed out the last vestiges of light from the building.

For a long time, none of the horses spoke. The silence lasted so long that the horse thought none of them would ever speak. It was only in the deepest rhythms of the night that one of them finally whispered:

'Are you staying?'

The horse's mind had wandered. He had been playing through the events that had brought him down from the hillside and thinking about what might lie ahead. So much so that he didn't hear the question, or at least dismissed it as another mewl in a disharmony of nightly noises.

The horse goaded his mind back to attention.

'Did one of you speak?' he asked.

'Are you staying?' the voice repeated.

'Staying?'

'You can't be staying here – can you? Not one like you.'

'One like me?'

'A moorlander don't have much use here – he must

be taking you somewhere. You can't be staying.'

The horse needed time to think. For some reason, he couldn't absorb it all and he felt out of place.

'A moorlander?'

'That's where you come from, ain't it?'

The horse thought.

'Yes.'

'Did he steal you? I bet he stole you, the crafty whip-master!'

'I … I don't know,' replied the horse.

They fell into a moment of silence.

'Well,' continued the voice, 'one thing's for sure, you ain't no dray horse.'

'You're saying I'm different?'

'You know it. This ain't no place for a wild pony. How d'you come by the devil? I'll bet he tricked you! I'll bet you anything you like, you was tricked!'

The voice exhaled his mirth.

The horse didn't know how to make sense of it, but now that his attention had returned, he wanted to seize on the conversation or respond in some way. A part of him bridled at the sardonic disdain the other horses showed towards him and wanted to challenge them. But he could also see that he didn't know enough to bring anything to the fight. As the outsider, he judged that it was better to hide all his thoughts. Instead, he tried to find out more.

'What is this place?' the horse asked simply.

Another pause. Were the other horses settled down for the evening?

'No place for you. That's something.'

'A farm,' said another voice.

It was the first time the third horse had said anything.

'Don't you worry,' said the first horse who had spoken, 'won't be no ridge and furrow for you.'

'No?'

'A courser, maybe. Who knows.'

In what remained of the night, the horse tried to make sense out of what had happened to him. He called to mind the path he had followed with the farmer – the route through the woodland and over the low-lying fields. He could remember a lot because all of it was so new.

The farm had been built into a flattened step in the hillside. From there, it was still possible to gaze out on the plain, but his descent brought with it a more limited sight of the horizon.

Had he done the right thing? Was this farmer somehow answering his response to the call he had received from the light on the horizon? Or had he been stolen? The horse was curious to know and understand more about the farm, but he knew, even on his first night there, that he didn't want to stay. He had left his home to go on a journey, to go in search of the light he had seen.

A sense of fear and foreboding came over him. Whether he had been tricked by the farmer was moot, but the farmer certainly had an ulterior motive. This motive cast a shadow over his instinct, intimating the true danger he was about to face. For all that, the horse's hunger to carry on, to see what was out there on the plain, remained. No such shadow, no unnerving prospect, made him think twice – at least, not seriously. If anything, the danger added more lustre to the enticing spectacle of the journey ahead.

Then he thought about his home. The moorland, the ridges, the grass commons scattered with ferns, the sudden escarpments, and the trace of the hills set against the evening – all of this was fresh in his mind, so much so that it was a place he still inhabited. To step into his memory was as simple as setting out through the door of the stables; but as he dozed in and out of sleep, it became more vivid. He trotted alone along the ridge until he caught a bird of prey pass over the silhouette of a cloud.

*

The next morning set the pattern for the weeks that would follow. First, a young man (not the farmer) would enter the stable to guide the other horses into the field, where he put them to work. A short while later the farmer would appear, his face a rosy smile, and take the horse out into an adjoining paddock.

The horse learned to trust the farmer and the farmer wanted the horse's trust, even though the designs on which this trust relied were unclear.

Over the farmer's shoulder the horse could see the other two horses leading a plough over a field that surmounted a gentle ridge. Their work was a steady act of meditation, a pattern that left its mark on the land. Neither of the horses complained. Neither of them looked weary. Neither of them, in their bearing or the fragments of conversation at the end of the day, gave any reason to think they resented their labour. Was this what the farmer intended for the horse?

However inscrutable the farmer's mind, the other two horses were adamant that he had no plan to put the horse to work in the fields. Certainly, the horse thought it would be an adjustment to adopt such a life. The freedom in which he had lived before had been absolute – he had never known any boundaries that would qualify his behaviour. Even so, the thought of a life as a farm horse didn't fill him with dread; he was even interested to experience it and interested to know why he wasn't repulsed by the idea of binding his daily existence to the material ambitions of the man before him. It was hard to explain without the experience and, in moments of frustration, he would burst into a run around the paddock.

'Does it hurt you?' the horse asked his companions one evening. 'Your work, I mean.'

'No, it doesn't hurt,' came the simple reply.

'Do you like it?'

But his companions didn't understand the question.

The more he watched his fellow creatures, the more he could see that these animals had a routine, a form, an order, that governed their lives. They were not free. They couldn't choose to do whatever they wanted. They were bound by their cycle of activity. In his former life, he could have done whatever he wanted but his life had no pattern or order. Was this where his restlessness came from?

One afternoon, the farmer came to the horse's paddock. In one hand he held an apple; in the other, a headcollar. At first, both arms stayed firmly at the farmer's side, and as the horse approached, the farmer pivoted the top half of his body over the fence. The horse reached the farmer and, in a way that had now become familiar, the farmer let his head rest on the horse's nose for a few seconds. The horse murmured as he imbibed the familiar smell. Then the farmer brought his body back to its full height, switched the halter to the same hand as the apple and with his free hand stroked and patted the horse about his nose. Calmly, the farmer brought the halter back to his free hand and, by way of extension to all the preceding movements, he fastened it to the horse's head. Once the job was complete, the farmer gave the horse the apple.

The horse could detect no trick. It felt – or it was made to feel – natural. He was pleased, even thrilled, by the newness of his strap. Even if the farmer had other plans for him, the horse was sure it prefigured a role of some kind, and with that thought came a rush of excitement. The farm was a world of sense, he had concluded after observing its fixtures and practices. It was a form of life adapted to nature. Just as the sun came and went each day, so the seasons changed. With them crops and cereals could be cultivated. The farmer and his retinue of workers measured their lives by these patterns and rhythms that, with care and hard work, bore fruit.

'What makes you so sure he don't have something else in mind?'

The horse had dared to whisper his thoughts to the

other horses one evening.

'Like what?' asked the horse, taking time to judge the question.

'There are other ways of living.'

The farmer soon completed his transformation of the horse. He brought forth a saddle and applied it with the same sugared sequence of movement. The sensation of carrying a rider, while new, was not intrusive or unpleasant. They began to trot around the paddock. Before long, the farmer dismounted, opened the paddock gate, guided the horse into the open and finally remounted. From there, the horse and his rider set out down a track beyond the furthest perimeter of the farm buildings and carried on at a canter into the unknown expanse of the plain.

They rode for many miles. It was a fine day, albeit touched by a chill. The sun, unsullied by cloud, broke through the sky. The horse enjoyed the use of his body for the first time in many days – all his muscles responded to the rider's command and the air swelled inside him.

The track led them through a land deserted save for livestock and the visible trace of wild animals. They only saw a handful of other people. Two were working on the land. Another was a semi-naked man trudging slowly and wearily down the same track. They passed through a wooded hillock before they turned sharply to the left. This road, which was lined on either side with trees, led to a large sprawl of buildings. As they drew nearer to it, they could see the place was teeming with people (and many other horses), all committed to their business.

The farmer took them on a course that circled the buildings and came to a series of large paddocks. Heads were beginning to turn. Then the farmer whistled, brought the horse to a slow trot, and approached a man, who carried himself with authority. This man, the horse came to learn, was a marshal, which meant that his authority derived from the command of horses.

The farmer and the marshal said very little to each other and what little they said concealed their true bent of mind; but their meeting was more than a pleasantry. A serious matter was at stake.

The marshal lingered at a distance, but his eyes flickered between the farmer and the horse, as he traced the outline of muscle and bone. The marshal was fascinated by what he saw. Outwardly, he was as thick-skinned as his first impression; but greed and calculation broke the veneer of his public appearance. He dusted down his hands.

The horse was sold in those brief moments. The details were only an extended gesture. The horse had, in a sense, been sold when the farmer first set eyes on him; one glance had beaten a path to the trade.

The marshal led the horse away.

*

In a fast moment, the horse considered what had happened to him. He had surrendered whatever wild and wayward portion of will he had known before to become a pawn in a trade between humans. The impression the other horses on the farm had imparted of the farmer – crafty, deceitful, opportunistic – appeared to have been borne out. Had he been duped? Should this have filled him with anger?

These thoughts, and others like them, made him cautious about what was happening to him, but for any warnings and despite his acquiescence to the calculations of one human after another, his curiosity outmanoeuvred everything. He was prepared to accept the trading and schemes of the men to whom he was temporarily bound, because – so far, at least – they had facilitated his journey. He had taken flight on their greed and narrow self-interest, and it had carried him further into the unknown territory of the plain. The horse still had no way to know if he was making a mistake, but he was prepared to take the risk.

Something tells me that you – all of you – will take me where I am meant to go.

His new stables were better kept and more ornate. They were also home to more horses than he could count and a small army of people attending to them, feeding them, washing, and grooming them, shoeing and dressing them. The horse had never imagined such a place – a place built just for the care and cultivation of his kind.

Then am I something special?

Before he was shut away for the night, the marshal's staff stripped him and scrubbed him down. He noticed the carefully hewn beams trimmed with equine patterns that seemed to set each part of the stable apart. These little embellishments, small as they were, suggested to the horse that the purpose of the place was more than practical; it didn't just exist to house the horses but to celebrate and glorify them.

'Are you ready?' came a voice nearby.

It was the horse in the stall next to him.

'Ready?' asked the horse.

'That's right; are you ready?'

'Ready for what?'

The horse waited for an answer from his neighbour.

'You'd better be ready,' he said eventually, and they said nothing more to each other for the rest of the night.

He spent the following morning grazing in the extensive paddocks. The stables, to his eyes, looked just as special and dignified from the outside. Beyond them, on the far side of a courtyard, he could see a fortified building, and around it were more buildings, many of them stables. It was also plain to see that a farrier worked under one of them.

This wasn't a farm – so much was clear. Some other purpose was at work.

Another man appeared – younger than any of the other men the horse had met so far. He stood upright, proud and a little haughty. He held the horse in his gaze, but the look stood apart from the way the farmer, or for that matter the marshal, had seen him. They had assessed his physique, studying every sinew and limb, as units that rounded to a pleasing sum. This man's eyes flowed with the grace of the horse's movements.

The horse approached the man slowly. When he got near enough, the horse lowered his head and the young man, without flinching or any detectable hesitation, reached out. Just like his gaze, the man's touch was unlike anything the horse had known before. The man's hands were hard, callused, but gentle; they strayed over the horse's nose with poise and direction, but guided by love. The young man leaned into the horse; the smell, for all its novelty, was familiar. Then the man whispered something in the horse's ear. The horse tried to understand what was at work between them; many things eluded him, including the young man's words.

The next day the horse was brought from his stable, saddled and guided out to the courtyard, where his new master stood waiting for him. As soon as he saw the horse, he unhooked a brooch that fastened an elegant green tunic, handed the garment to an older man at his side, picked up a lance and strode forwards.

Once more the young man stood upright, shoulders wide, and stared into the horse's eyes. Then, in a single movement, he mounted the horse. The horse stayed perfectly still, untroubled by the weight. The small group of people assembled around them were surprised. Some of them gasped; they had expected something else, either an unsettled horse or an unsettled rider – possibly both.

The horse, for his part, met his new rider with more than calculated passivity. There was something special about this young man; he had felt it under the touch of his hands the day before, and could sense it stronger still as his mount. A connection was forming between them and binding them fast. The horse didn't just go along with it to see where it would take him; he was invigorated by a sense of promise and a new spark of life.

They set out at pace across the courtyard, through

an archway and out into the country. The horse could sense the heat in the young man's belly; it stirred their speed.

They carried on in this fight of forward movement until something caught the eye of the young man. He pulled hard on the horse's reins, and they came to a halt. They were looking over a stretch of open land to their right where, in the distance and at the boundary of woodland, another creature was standing as silent as a statue. They turned and proceeded towards the animal at a slow trot.

The deer didn't frighten. It lowered its head, walked curiously a little way over the land, then turned on itself where it found a way into the trees. The rider didn't react to the deer or show any concern that it might elude their trail. They kept to the same slow, steady pace across the open land and into the woods.

The horse knew what the rider wanted. His only role was to keep the same pace. They were not giving chase – not yet. Neither did they want to startle or frighten their quarry. They followed a wide track through the woodlands. On either side of them the forest floor was strewn with wildflowers. Moss layered rocks and boulders and the long limbs of creepers fragmented what they could see all about them. They trod carefully through a spread of dog's mercury and bluebells, passing the portly trunks of beech trees.

The rider tested everything with his eyes: the branches and leaves for any signs of displacement, and the ground for tracks. A sound came to them from somewhere. Their pace slowed. This wasn't the burst of animal energy they had shared before, but in its conviction, it was just as powerful.

Their path took a gentle turn to the right, at the instruction of a fallen branch. The horse and its rider squeezed around a narrow gap, where they stopped. The deer was standing, just off to the right in a small clearing. It was staring at them. Its thin neck reached up from its body and the delicate daub of its head didn't flex or twitch.

Until now, the horse hadn't deviated from the task he and his master had undertaken. The horse looked into the eyes of the creature and, in an instant, he was lost; he no longer knew where he was or what he was doing. A thin film of fear pushed at the surface of the deer's eyes – an involuntary and instinctive reaction of its body that, in the right circumstances, kept it attuned to danger. Beneath the surface, running its course beyond the diversions of life and death, was something else: a spirit, unless it was a memory as old, ancient and beautiful as the form that had temporarily brought it life.

He wanted to call to the hart, but the creature lowered its head. Then the horse felt the contortion of his rider's body and heard the whisper of his master's lance through the air. The weapon pierced the deer through its neck. The ripple of fear gathered into a wave of panic and terror, as the animal staggered forwards and sideways, until it surrendered its life to the ground a little way ahead of them, just to the side of the forest track. The forest was silent.

The same fear the horse had seen in the eyes of the hunted animal, sounded in a sympathetic echo through the sinewy courses of his body. In a different circumstance he might have shied or run, but he knew what was required of him, and the intensity and purpose of his master's action willed him to stand firm.

The hunters watched the animal die, the same heightened senses knowing, if not yet accepting, the achievement of their goal. The rider knew it before the horse and dismounted to claim his prize. He led the horse forward by the rein. The horse could see, at close quarters, that the outline of the deer concealed its strength and agility; they were intruding on a secret that the creature would, in life, have always kept to itself. Something about these animals never wanted to be seen completely. As if to respect this wish, the horse and the man kept as quiet as they could and worked with care to carry their victim home. The horse was struck again by the deer's eyes. The life had gone out of them, but its traces were still there to see – whatever he had seen in them would never allow an observer to get this close without forfeiting its life.

The situation stirred up so many strange thoughts and associations. He couldn't wrestle sense out of the moment. Seeing the bloody corpse of the animal immediately recalled his – increasingly distant – memory of the dead horse he had seen on the moorland. Except this time he had been complicit in the act of violence, and the unsteady instinct to flee, whinny, frighten and run, was now controlled by custom – a dead animal was no longer a cause for alarm but something like a regular occurrence. The horse knew that he would see other dead animals, and that their appearance would count as a sobering consequence of the life he had chosen.

The proximity to death was also deadening, as if it cauterised his sensitivity to its offence and curbed the limits of life itself. It confirmed the fears he had partially intuited when he had deliberated about his choice to leave the hillside. He was losing something; the innocence and freedom in which he had wandered the hills had been sharpened into the shape of a finite form and bound to the life of other creatures. For all that, and so much was made clear in the brutal certainty of his new

Lord and master, a kind of vitality, spirit and definition came from the bloody business, as if the compressed competition for life lent it new force and character. His journey from the moors had cost him the freedom and peace he had known, but put something new in its place.

And I want to know more of it.

*

The horse's new master trained the horse on many similar exercises, none as memorable as their first hunt for the deer. They had ridden slowly, even sadly, with the corpse of the killed animal draped across the horse's rear. It chilled him to feel the dead creature on his body and the trickle of its blood around his haunches. Life might have gone from it, but something lingered, haunting their return and reminding them of the bargain into which they had entered.

Horse and master came to know each other – their shared movements, intentions, moods, and calculations. In the time that followed, they travelled alone and as part of organised hunting parties, straddled by groundsmen, gamekeepers, and dogs. If he had to be ready for something, was this it? For all its exhilaration, he was sure that this sport was only a preparation. None of the other animals said so, but their manner assumed as much.

Then their play became a mission. The horse and his master set out from the marshal's quarters with a sense not of training or an effort to refine the instincts of conflict, but in pursuit of business. His rider even looked different and it was plain enough from the pride and purpose of his carriage that the task they were about to discharge was important.

They followed the same road over the open land, retracing the terrain of their recent hunt. This time the journey continued for the rest of the day, until the rider took his rest at an inn. The next day they kept going. If the horse had any sense of geography, it had been fashioned only by his home in the hills and the long horizon of the plain. This journey appeared to trace his old home because he could see the unsteady shape of the land bobbing in the distance to his left. Where the road led, he couldn't know, but if anything, the place became more unkept and wild the further they advanced. For the first two nights, his master found lodgings, food and sustenance, but from the third night, they slept in the open country, tended only by an open fire.

After four days solid riding, the master guided them on a gentle route into the hills. Except these weren't the hills the horse had known; the high bluffs and vertiginous shadows of rock had become gentle undulations, rising occasionally to a high top from which the land around could be surveyed. It was up one of these natural watching places that his master led them. At the crest of the hill, they came to a stone hunting lodge fortified by thick walls and a perimeter dug out to serve as a moat but without any water. The rider dismounted, tied the horse loosely to an ash tree and went into the building.

The horse waited. It was silent all about. There wasn't even a small settlement or hamlet nearby to service the lodge. The only sound that broke his total seclusion was the gentle patter of rain and the occasional rustle of leaves above him. Something was not right.

His wait lasted longer than he knew how to calculate. It was broken only by a distant cry somewhere on the far side of the lodge. By instinct, the horse shuffled backwards and found, to his surprise, that the rein his rider had apparently used to bind him came loose. The horse, swayed by an unformed course of action, took a few steps to his left.

Another sharp and stifled bark cried out. The horse cantered in a circuit along the ridge of the moated site. Above him and to his right, he could see the movements of two sentries. They had seen the horse and were calling to someone about it. The horse quickened and caught up with the source of the commotion.

His young Lord was suspended from one of the windows two-thirds of the way up the stonework, straining and struggling at the end of a rope. With his two free hands he was doing all he could to free its bind from his neck, but the blood was starting to surface on his face and his mouth could only manage panicked gasps of air. For all that, he saw the horse straight away. His eyes, with the same desperate stirrings of life, rushed at him, and as their eyes met, the horse also received a peculiar sensation that something was about his neck and he could no longer breathe. The horse formed the thought that unless he did something, unless he acted now, the choking sensation would steal his breath altogether.

The horse scaled the bank of the moat and churned its boggy base; he climbed the bank on the far side and sidled up to the wall of the building, so that he could become his master's seat. The legs of the young knight gripped his torso and the horse's back eased into the familiar weight. Quickly, the young man freed himself from the noose and took the two of them to flight. Missiles – rocks, dung and other detritus – were starting to rain.

On the far side of the moat, they wasted no time. They stopped only to glance at their assailants. Men were gathered on the ramparts of the lodge; one had resorted to hurling abuse and another was reaching for a bow and quiver. Against the shuttered window from which his knight had been left to hang, they could just see the dark shape of a figure shifting against the daylight.

Whatever the nature of the knight's journey, it had failed. He made no further entreaties in the stone keep; his violent reception was decisive enough and suggested that his diplomatic purpose – if that's what it was – had been ill-judged. Horse and rider returned the way they had come, picking a route in the shadow of the hills (the horse, as they travelled, thought he could detect them calling to him).

At the end of their first day's flight, they settled down to camp. The knight made a fire, and the two creatures regarded each other on either side of the dim light. The knight would look up at the horse sheepishly. The horse shuffled about, occasionally making snorting noises, eager to know his master's mind.

Before long, the master spoke. His voice was hoarse and rasped over the air and smoke between them. He spoke only a few brief words but they were clearly directed at the horse. A visible bruise had burgeoned around his neck. His face was swollen and distorted by the trauma of his experience. The horse had no idea what the knight was saying.

The knight spoke again, this time looking the horse squarely in the face. The horse let the words come then fade, before he made his own abortive attempt at a reply with a loud exhalation of breath. The horse looked at the young man, and then at his damaged neck. It was easy to see that a fire was at work in him. Even with the scars of his near-fatal experience, the same temper was unsettled beneath the surface and visible in the manner and character of his body. The horse snorted again and the knight gave a one-word reply.

It was the knight's steel, drive, determination or undaunted resolve to which the horse could relate. It was the same resolve, the same will, that had stirred him into being and brought him out of the wilderness. Could the knight see it?

The knight spoke again.

Was that a reply? The horse thought.

The knight, a little uneasy on his legs, stood and took a careful course around the fire. There, he patted the horse, rubbed his nose and whispered words.

*

It happened before long. The day began in a different way. The entire company of the marshal's office set out with purpose. They wore different clothes. The horse's master appeared in chain mail and a helmet. His squire draped the horse in an ornate caparison. The company came together quickly – everyone was eager to set out. The horse had never seen so many men and horses in one place. They rode onto the road.

The horse had only a faint sense of the land, and while he couldn't say where exactly they were, he knew he was travelling further into the plain. This thought alone would have stirred his energies, but in concert with the new life he had found, it dazzled him, just like the light he had seen from afar. The workhorses on the farm had been right; he was not suited to their life. Even if he couldn't recognise it himself, they had taken one look at him and, just like the farmer, they saw his character. His former restlessness, the call of the light on the horizon – they had led him to this moment.

The cavalry rode for most of the morning until they spied an encampment of men within striking distance of a town that had been built on a gentle incline in the land. Two concentric walls marked out the shape of the town; the outer wall protected a serried settlement of timber-framed houses, clustered over the terrain, like a crop of spring flowers. The inner wall hemmed a spoilt decoration at the crest of a hill; a castle still smarting from its wounds, as a long trail of black smoke left it partially obscured.

The castle and the town were the target. How long the assaulting army had been staking out their enemy, the horse couldn't tell, but impatience was in the air.

No-one could sit still and anger, unchecked by court-ly manners, simmered beneath the surface. The men were visibly angry – they scowled, swore, shouted and eyed their weapons. This was not just an army of professional soldiers steeling themselves for battle. They were aggrieved; and the injustice – which anyone who looked could read – sharpened their blades more than the industry of any blacksmith. Whatever had happened to them, the penalty had been heavy. Was the town and its keep rightfully theirs?

'Yes,' said one of the other horses. 'Yes, you guess correctly. Many of the men you see before you were stationed at the castle. It was taken from them. Rumour is that many of the townsfolk have since been mistreated.'

The horse stayed silent.

'The men hereabouts have been trying to muster a force to mount a counterattack for many months. It seems their time has come.'

'Then their time is ours.'

'Yes.'

The horse turned his attention to the castle and the slow-burning fire that was the source of the plume.

'They keep the flame burning. So that the defeated are reminded of their humiliation. We will see blood. Soon enough, we will see blood.'

The other horse was hastened away.

Anything was possible in the current atmosphere; the anger might overspill in any direction and engulf whatever it found. Another rider on another caparisoned mount rode out before the line of horsemen, and in shouting distance of the encampment. He held his sword high. He shouted a single word several times. The first call caught the attention of the assembly, the second was answered by a murmur, and the third by a violent bark of shared intention.

The rider had just begun the overtures of a martial speech when he was interrupted by a yell from behind him. The entire entourage of the cavalry and soldiery diverted their attention. They saw a figure stumbling down from the town's main gate, where he staggered about beneath the walls. The horse caught a rusty choke of laughter from one or two of the knights near him. As he looked a little more closely, he could see that the yelling man who had emerged from the enemy's battlements was naked from the waist down and waving his private parts in their direction. He also carried a large ale jug. The man turned around and bent forward, bearing his arse at the besieging army.

The men around the horse were muttering. Their stiff laughter had turned to frowns and indignation. The caparisoned rider, who had been about to launch into an address, shouted over the field at the drunk semi-naked man, which led other men to lend their own voices to a chorus of cries and insults. This did nothing to temper the drunk man's behaviour. He only taunted the army further. The mood grew more tense. A soldier from the camp walked forward brandishing his sword, shouting abuse at the drunkard. Another soldier pulled a dagger and went through the empty gesture of cutting off his own genitals, which occasioned a soft ripple of laughter from those around him.

The humour vanished at the sound of a much louder clarion call from inside the city walls. The army held its collective breath, as a sortie of riders came out waving arms, lances, swords, and flags. They shouted death at the men coming to reclaim their territory.

The hatred among the besiegers swelled. With no coordination, no rousing speeches or tactical sleight of hand, the rider who had been waving his sword at the undressed man, charged at the advancing sortie. Lone horseman and soldiers followed his example, like the first loose rocks at the advance of a landslide. Then the whole army mobilised in an outraged and indignant lurch at the audacity of their enemy. Those about the horse grabbed anything to hand (the horse even saw one man grab a branding iron), so great was the will to fight.

The horse, too, was caught up in it all. Their pain

and their righteous anger touched everyone. He also knew that the smoking ruin of the castle was the end point of his journey. It was the light he had seen, the signal, the call, that had brought him out from the wild. This battle was the last, and culminating, step towards his goal.

Fury stirred the blood in his veins, and a great sweeping swell of danger washed through his body, threatening to burst through his heart and mouth. His legs pounded the earth. His mouth snarled at the riders before him, as if he and the monstrous charge to which he belonged were trying to swallow them whole.

Go! Flee! Die!

The army collided with their enemy in a brutal explosion that annihilated all before them. The pretence of a fight on equal terms was short-lived. His rider swiped off the head of one foe in a single blow. The horse snarled, biting at men, and other horses, as he choked through the fog of battle. The forward charge of the cavalry cut through the defending sortie from the city; and, as if propelled by a force they had unleashed but which they could no longer control, they stormed through the city gates and rampaged through the streets, unchecked by physical or moral constraints. Soldier after soldier fell before them. The horse's rider cut off limbs, severed arteries, at one point drove his sword by way of the eye socket clean through the skull of his victim, and spilled the brain matter of another onto the cobbled streets. The siege, blinded by blood, careered out of control until there was no more blood to spill. No-one was spared: young, old, man or woman.

The battle lasted little more than a couple of hours, after which time the besieging army disbanded into a sated stupor of death. The horse and his rider trotted slowly through the streets, the uncivil remains of their violence all about them, until they settled before the castle. The rider dismounted. Leading the horse by the reins, he approached the castle walls. When he was close enough, he placed the palm of his hand on the stonework.

The horse bowed his head – he had answered the voice that had called him.

*

In the time that followed, the horse was kept busy with the military business of his master; but in the rare moments of respite from their duties, he tried to learn more about the keep that had called to him. He still didn't understand the nature of what was at work. Was there an individual in the building, a sorcerer hidden away, who had orchestrated the signal? Or was it more subtle than that?

Unlike his master, he was never allowed inside the building, even if he was often stabled nearby. The conquering army had extinguished the flame in the tower, and it was evident that they were now exerting the same energy to restore and rebuild it with as much speed and resolution as their invasion.

'What is the tower?' he asked one evening in the stables.

'What is it?'

'Is it something special?'

'It's surely that. But who can say?'

'Has anyone been inside? Any horse, I mean?'

'Only by way of a spit, I'd fancy.'

'So none of us have seen it living?'

'I'll bet one of those Lords was so minded with madness that he would have admitted a horse to keep his company. But that would be before my time, or the time of any horse you'll find here.'

'A pity.'

'Let it lie. Know your station.'

But the horse couldn't let it lie. A small army of men hummed with activity about the keep. Stonemasons, carpenters, and the regular congress of lords, ladies and servants meant that it was never simply left to silence. Had all these people arranged the call? Was it a signal sent out across the land, so that creatures and men might rally to their cause? And yet, when he had first seen the light – dim though it now was in his memory – he had no knowledge of these people, their business and their cause, so how could it effect in him that sort of loyalty? In which case was the light something else, a signal from somewhere or someone else? What did it want from him?

'How old is it?' he asked.

'Older than me, I can tell you that.'

'Does it belong to someone?'

'A lord, I'd say. And no doubt he owes some allegiance to a king.'

'Has it always existed?'

'These places exist for a reason, and that reason took shape around the land. I couldn't say it's as old as the hills, but its reason derives from them.'

The horse laboured in vain to elicit any more substantial information from the other horses. They knew no or little more than he did. Unlike the horse, they showed no interest in the tower and its history. They soon tired of his questioning and refused to respond to him with anything more than the most truncated and unfriendly answers. Which left the horse to his own speculations and imaginings.

One night he just caught the ghost of a man walking by the entrance to the stables. The horses snorted, trying to catch the ghost's attention. He thought it had wandered away from him, when it materialised, crouched on the ground, a barely discernible outline clinging to the form it had lost. On closer examination, he could see that the figure was a boy rather than a man, and one of his eyes had been put out.

'I think you wanted to talk to me,' said the boy.

One or two of the horses exhaled and one voice called out quietly *Leave us alone!*.

'How long have you been here?' asked the horse.

'It's hard to say,' said the boy.

'Have you always lived here?'

'For a long time.'

'I wanted to know more about the keep.'

The boy looked at the horse.

'You come from far away. You come from the hills.'

The horse blinked. He didn't know how to take the boy's observation.

'I think the keep called me here.'

'A keep can do no calling. It's made of stone.'

'Then something in the keep called me.'

'What then?'

'There was a fire.'

'That's a recent business.'

'I only came here recently.'

'Do you find it to your liking?'

'Who built the tower?'

'It was built long ago. Does anyone remember?'

'Then even you don't know?'

'Why should I know?'

'I just wanted to know what called me.'

'Maybe it was something inside yourself. That called you, I mean. Perhaps it called you and made you grow. You are a fine horse. Anyone can see it. Even I can.'

'It felt like a light called me.'

'You can hold a light inside yourself.'

'But can you see it?'

'After a manner of speaking.'

Leave us alone! called out the voice in the stables again.

'Does a sorcerer live in the castle?'

The boy laughed.

'There are no sorcerers here.'

'I don't understand it.'

The ghost stood up, or shifted his shape into a different form.

'Perhaps you could see two lights and they wanted to become one.'

'What do you mean?'

'I should leave you alone. You horses don't like me. Apparently. Except for you of course. You, it seems, are the exception.'

'I am no stranger to spirits.'

'They run freely in the hills, I suppose.'

The boy disappeared.

Then, at another time, the horse and his master were trotting slowly along the banks of a river that cut out the shape of a valley through the rise of hills on either side of it. His master was unusually quiet, almost *neutral*; no objective guided them and no will set their course. His knight, but for the gentle weight of him, might just as easily not have been there. The horse was left with an uneasy feeling that the knight had vacated his customary role so that the horse might lead the way, that the situation for all its banality, required him to show some initiative.

Except there was nothing to give the horse cause. To what was he meant to respond? The natural delights of the valley? These were plentiful enough and, in their more understated way, perhaps they deserved a response, but it was not one the horse knew how to give and was entirely foreign to the business his rider had taught him to know. There were no other people. There weren't even any animals. Still, something was drawing them on, waiting to be discovered.

The horse, taking the same uncomfortable lead, followed the grassy banks of the river, as it broached a large bend. The land had pressured the river into the vertiginous slopes of the hill, creating on their side a large area of pasture, flat and unspoiled by the encroachment of trees. It was clear to see that the river, when it swelled, had fought back against the presumptions of the land and flooded the field, creating pockets of floodwater. But the river threatened no immediate flood – it had sunk into itself, exposing the silty mud concealed by its usual level. Sun broke around the hillside, catching the leaves on the trees that canopied the hills about them. Altogether it was a peaceful scene, one that brooked no discomfort and invited no obvious challenge.

Then the horse saw the movement of something other than the long grasses and branches of trees caught in a gentle breeze. A figure was standing with their back to them on some sort of coracle. He held firmly to a large staff that he had skewered into the mud on the far shore so that he might anchor his craft against the slow current of the water. The horse and his master continued their languorous journey, but the horse's attention was now fixed to the man.

The figure was small, not much more than a child and the closer they came the horse entertained the thought that it might be the same ghost he had quizzed about the keep – but it was hard to tell.

The horse came closer still, so that they were now

almost standing directly opposite each other on either bank of the river. The boy, apparently aware that he was no longer alone, dispensed with his struggle to moor his boat. He stood still for a moment. Then he turned around.

Even from the front, it was hard to know for sure if the boy was the same boy he had seen in the stables. It was a boy though – so much was clear, but the details of his features were hard to make out. Indeed, now that the horse looked properly, the boy's face was impenetrable – it would admit no human feature but disassembled into a sort of blur.

Suddenly, the boy extended his right hand in a gesture to halt the horse. The horse obeyed and awaited further instruction. Words came from the boy, but the horse was at pains to distinguish them and their sense. He could hear they were words, and he knew the boy was speaking, and speaking to him, but, like the boy's face, they were unclear.

Then the horse felt a sensation deep in his chest. It began as a warm glow, then grew into a burst of burning. Uncannily, the horse was not distressed, except enough to look down, from where he could just feel the heat at the surface of his body and witness the rippling edges of a flame. A ball of fire cut through him and floated like a large ember in the sunshine. The horse held it in his gaze, watching it rise in the air and float out a little way above the water, before it began to sink. It fell beneath the riverbank, until it came to rest just above the waterline. There it hovered for a while, until it sank beneath the surface of the river. But the flame didn't extinguish – the horse could see it burnishing and flickering as strong and bright as before.

The horse knew at this point to let his gaze return to the boy. Like the horse, the boy had held the flame with his attention, but now he turned it back to the horse, and in not more than a moment, he yanked his staff from the mud, freeing the coracle into the rustling pace of the river. The boy, and with him the flame under the water, sailed downstream. The horse watched them take their leave, until he was seized by a need to follow them, at which point he began to run.

He ran across the remaining stretch of pasture, desperate to find out where the boy was going, until he came to a track that cut through trees that leaned dangerously over the waters. Between their trunks, the horse could just make out the flame and the coracle forging ahead.

The river ran in another long arc and the horse was at pains to keep pace with the boy and the flame under the water. Emerging from the woodland, into another open field, he just caught the object of his pursuit disappearing beyond the next bend. He set out at full speed, but when he reached the sharp point of the bend, he could see that the boy and the flame had vanished completely. The river widened into an estuary that met another much larger river. Perched above a rocky outcrop at the confluence of waters, was a magnificent castle. It stood high above the water, exploiting the vantage point and guarding the waterways with an ominous and forbidding eye. The castle was so imposing and stationed above such a precipitous descent that it looked impregnable – except for the fact that it was burning. A great flame billowed from its summit that made it look more like a giant torch.

The horse was sure that the burning castle was the same keep he and his rider had stormed in their first skirmish. But the geography about them was entirely different. Now that the horse stopped to consider the matter, he didn't even know how he had come to be in the valley in the first place.

The horse stood still. He watched the castle burn.

At another time, he recalled this displaced adventure in the company of the dead young boy he had spoken to before.

'Was it you?' he asked. 'The boy in the boat I saw. Were you leading me somewhere?'

'It wasn't me. It's a strange account though. I even

wonder if it's real.'

'It felt real enough.'

'And, of course, a shadow casts its shape by the light of something real.'

'What do you mean?'

'Who is to say what is *only* a shadow? A commanding view is always limited by natural horizons.'

'These sound like riddles. And I don't know what you mean.'

'I am a ghost. To you I seem real. To others – maybe not. So maybe the temptation is to scatter *what is* under the feet of your own forward trudge. And the function of a riddle, by such a way of thinking, would only be to make everything look like shadows, so that, in the final account, every shadow stands in the same light.'

'What *is* the light? What was the fire that came out of me? It's the same, I know it. It's the same as the fire I saw here burning up each castle.'

'How did you come to be here?'

The horse halted, his mind trapped between his struggle with what he had seen and an answer to the question, and when he tried to tackle the question, he found that the memory he had so firmly known was no longer there, at least not there with the same clarity and definition. He knew he had come from the hills, but his memory of them had become more attenuated and diffuse, as if he were reaching to describe an abstraction, a concept or a feeling distilled into its purest state. Then a detail came to mind.

'I saw a bird,' he said.

'A bird?'

'An unusual one. One I had never seen before.'

'Birds, they say, are messengers.'

'Then you're saying the bird was a spirit who was guiding me towards the fire in this castle.'

'It's a handsome conclusion.'

'Why would a bird want me to come here?'

'Spirits have their ways.'

'How do you know these things?'

'I had some learning. When I was alive.'

'A pity, then, that you're dead.'

'That's also my view.'

'But if you know so much, tell me – what is the fire?'

'You came here from the hills. There you were carrying a flame inside yourself. The great billowing flame you saw here called to your inner flame, by way of mutual attraction. So that flame you carry inside yourself might be seen; let me be plain – so that you might be seen. So that you might discover what you can become.'

'Is *that* it?'

'A light will always cause things to be seen.'

*

It was clear to the horse that he had been destined for battle. His body, his physique, his instincts, and the swirl of feelings that attended them, were not just suited to war, but reached their peak in its clamour. He didn't question it, doubt it, or want to change it – he just knew it. He could only see what he had become: a knight's mount. The light in the tower had drawn him out of nothing. The more he embraced this vocation, the fainter his memory of his former life and home became, to the point that it was so diffuse as to seem unreal. In any case, it didn't matter. All that mattered was the life he had found.

This life was, without doubt, a brutal and dangerous one, but he was well-treated, groomed and even revered. He and his rider knew and understood each other, and the nature of their calling. They faced death and the cruellest violence wherever they went and gifted both to those about them. But this danger and violence held the highest value because it carried with it the exercise of power. With every charge they brokered a relationship with the world around them.

In the time after the siege, the entire company of the marshal's horses and their riders took up – or returned to – residence in the city. From there they rode out onto the plain to fight other battles. In the first few skirmishes, they rode for more than a day, and after they had secured these victories, they rode for several days, camping out in the open or setting up camp at smaller fortified postings.

His knight, it seemed, was at war and with the reconquest of the castle, he had turned it to his advantage. The other horses spoke, albeit sparingly, and confirmed as much, but the horse had no need for their words – he knew it all from the bearing of his master. The knight didn't take pleasure in the act of war for its own sake – he had an end in sight that he was pursuing with a force of will that propelled everyone towards it.

His bent of mind would yield nothing to his enemies, to the complaints and fears of his fellow warriors, to the horse, and perhaps most of all, to himself; the knight would die fighting his way to victory.

They fought in the open fields; they mounted a surprise attack from woodland, crushing an off-guard remnant of infantry; they forded a river and cut the line of a large army in two. The rider hacked flesh to pieces, like a farmer harvesting wheat. The horse became familiar with the splash of blood on his hair and in his eyes, with cuts and slashes at his body.

The horse, time and again, walked a fine line between life and death, but the danger and intensity of battle brought him alive in ways that he had never thought possible. He had never felt such a heady and intoxicating rush of raw power as when he took part in a charge, the swelling cry and thunderous wall of noise raising the pitch of his blood. At any moment, he thought it might overtake him and pull the earth from beneath his feet.

He never tired of these battles, any more than the rider; but after they had waged war for many months, the horse noticed that their enemies were losing each battle, so much so that the number of conflicts started to wither away.

The knight and the army with which he fought must have achieved their aim. They had not only re-taken their citadel but consolidated the terrain for many miles around. They had established themselves as *the author-ity* to which everyone in the area owed allegiance. And in the time they had prosecuted their cause, the horse had noticed how the once tarnished and battle-worn castle they had relieved in their first siege had trans-formed. It had been rebuilt, extended with a new cur-tain wall and bailey. Men and women milled about it, their service binding the building – and the donjon in particular – with lustre and magnificence.

The city was a source of admiration, and the pride placed in its central building cascaded down to the many smaller lodgings, workshops and taverns that had burgeoned after the city's sacking. The place whistled with life.

For all the apparent victory the knight had won, the horse never sensed triumph in his rider. The horse was even tempted to conclude that his knight had not yet reached his coveted goal; or that the knight's goal was to die in battle.

When he had first been sold to the marshal, the horse had been prepared to accept the machinations of his human masters, however venal and opportunistic they might have been. They had brought him out of the empty lands he had once known. Any yet his relationship with the knight had become something more. He admired, even loved, him. The reason was simply that, without him, the horse would not have found his place, his character, the point of the animal instinct that had carried him out of the wild. Their bond was, however, more than an unfeeling contrivance; they shared an instinct and the unsmiling act of will his master displayed led the way with a sense of direction the horse knew and understood, even if he couldn't see far enough to spy where it might take them.

The authority they brought imbued a fervour and fight in the pair of them, as if it was a higher power before which they lay prostrate. Just as their brutal business had found the horse's character and helped him to display the order and poise he had previously only sensed, so it brought identity to the world around them. The once ruined keep was now resplendent and proud; but the settlements, towns, hamlets, and dwellings that had been the pitch for their martial sport, were gradually melding, reshaping and converging to discover their own order and poise. Merchants and their carts trod out the roads between these places, minstrels and beggars felt less inhibition about setting out on foot, villagers returned to maypoles and a little later they burned bones at festivals of fire.

This strange authority – strange because it came by way of such violence – felt to the horse like an unseen character, manifest all around them yet more elusive than the sum of its parts. The horse knew that, even if the knight was not looking to give his life in battle, he would gladly do so. So much followed from everything they had done together. If they conferred death on those around them for a greater good, then it was unreasonable and dishonourable to expect they might be excluded from the cost. The horse also knew that where his rider went, he must follow.

*

The knight was pushing too hard. Set piece battles, routs and skirmishes all continued but they diminished in scale and significance. They even became easier. The enemy put up less of a fight, knowing they were defeated. Except the knight was not satisfied; if an enemy yielded too easily, it only engorged his anger, as if he was frustrated by the lack of resistance. The young man, the horse thought, wanted it all to continue when it had bruited about every part of the land that the war had reached its conclusion.

On one of their last journeys into battle, the knight gathered a small retinue and set out on an expedition that lasted some days. It was only on the day before they reached their destination that the horse recognised where they were; the features of the land resembled the journey he and his master had undertaken alone, not long before their first battle. And sure enough, the following day their company marched into sight of the same hunting lodge where his knight had very nearly been neck-stretched to lasting silence.

The building was the same; the moat was dry save for the small pools that had collected after recent rainfall. The military force spent a short while reconnoitring the building, but they wasted no time in besieging the isolated stronghold.

The ramshackle collection of armed individuals who were defending the lodge could see their time had come; to pre-empt the siege – and observe the honour of the battlefield – they lowered the portcullis and came fully armed and on horseback at the besieging force. Unusually, each rider was hooded and carried a large flaming torch, which meant their features could not be seen. The purpose of wielding fire was not clear to the attacking force but they all saw it as something out of the ordinary that prefigured a manoeuvre of some kind. They looked about them – including over their shoulders – for the signs of deception or an ambush.

The knight rallied his men and they went to meet the defensive assault. At first the besieged riders did nothing with their torches. This only frustrated the knight's men. The horse could feel a hateful swell of anger rise inside his master and then, at a pitch of violence that caught the ear of everyone, he shouted at the fire-carrying riders. A figure, responding to the rebuke, rode towards the horse and his master. He called out his own hot reply before coming nearer. It was just possible to make out the scarred remains of his face.

When he was near enough, his gaze settled on the horse with a look of loathing. In service to it, he swung the torch in his left hand so that it flashed over the nose and eyes of the horse. The heat burnt into his eyes and he could feel the tips of his hair curl and crisp under direct influence of the heat. The knight tried to control his animal but it was too late. The horse reared up with a terrified whinny, throwing his rider from the saddle. In this position, something hard struck him on his side, and as his forelegs returned to earth, he staggered sideways, where he met the edge of the moat. He stumbled and rolled down the embankment, coming to an indecorous mess at its base.

There, he lay, shocked into paralysis and expecting a final blow to despatch him. He didn't know if, or how badly, he was injured or even how long he was lying in his state of moribund indignity. He could still hear noises; the clarion call of voices and the cold clash of swords.

Then someone was about him. Unless he was much mistaken, they had straddled their legs about his head and leaned down so that they might press their head into his. At the first shift of movement, he had assumed that it would be an assailant come to deliver on the promise of death; but as soon as he felt the touch of their skin, he knew it was his master. Words came. They were muttered straight into his ear with a haste and urgency he was meant to feel. And this time, in the delirious torment of the moment, he could torment a little sense from them.

'Come, my creature,' he said. 'Come now.'

And that was all it needed. Blood surged and the competition returned. The fight was about him and he wanted to see it done; most of all he wanted to wrench the fire from the hand of the figure who had seared his coat and complete the partial injury left on his enemy's body.

They were on their feet again. His master rode the rising of his animal, so they were reunited in their return to full stature. The rider spurred them to action, but the horse needed no encouragement. They gathered up the steep embankment of the moat and rejoined the fracas.

The bodies of men lay about them. Some of the torches were burning out on the ground. His knight gave a whistle, and by way of acknowledgement, one of his men picked up one of the flames and handed it to the knight. Somehow, even slowly, they picked a passage through the dwindling scene of carnage until they found the hated figure with his back to them and engaging in an act of martial murder. With a gentle inclination of his head, the horse leaned forward so that the rider could lean over him; and in this position, he put the torch to the foot of the figure's robe.

Then came a second whistle. The hooded figure turned. The knight met this motion with a swing of his sword and cut straight through his combatant's arm. The victim screamed and reached to nurse his injury with his remaining hand, by which time he was too late to realise that he was fully ablaze, fast becoming the brightest torch on the field of conflict and the screaming candle that brought the slaughter to an end.

The knight's retainers spent a little while plundering the lodge and a small number were instructed to remain, where they would consolidate the building. But most of the company left the way they had come.

Later that afternoon, they set up camp amidst a small copse of yew trees, where they made a fire and took some rest. The knight approached the horse, examining him from the front and then each side. A portion of the hair on the bridge of his nose had been burned away. The horse could just catch the blackened edges of the patch it had left. His knight examined the area but was apparently looking for something more – an effect or frightened habit it had left on him, perhaps. But the horse was not frightened, and he was quick to show it in the look he returned to his master. It was pleasing to see that this intention was understood; his master ran the callused palm of his hand down the horse's muzzle.

Show me the fire, the horse wanted to say. *Let me feel it again.*

*

As war gave way to peace, other activities soon took the place of killing. The horse had expected they might return to hunting; but this only figured at the margins of their peacetime activity. Instead, they took up a proxy war, a game that other horses and animals knew by the name of the joust. In this game, a rider, armed with a blunted lance and shield, would ride at an opponent, each with the aim of unseating the other. Many young men took part in the festivities; some came from miles around. The competition and pride that fuelled the spectacle, drew crowds, and led to daring feats of entertainment. The rider, to the amusement of his onlookers, boasted a special trick, whereby he would dodge his opponent's lance, grab their stirrups to unseat them, then lead them on a humiliating circuit of the tiltyard.

He and his master took part in the joust infrequently but with devastating ferocity. The mood of the tournament changed as soon as they took their places. Where the crowd had been jubilant, goading, shouting, cheering – and as often laughing – at the participants, they turned sombre and silent. They applauded when he won, but they didn't revel in the moment as they did with the other horsemen. They watched their admiration carefully.

The joust, while nothing like war, was still dangerous. Riders were injured or killed, and their steeds could be badly hurt or maimed. His master disgorged his animal drive into each charge, and, for a brief moment, they recreated the terrifying thunder of the battlefield. Even so, it was only a semblance of war, an approximation securely bound in a safe-making code of conduct. His master wanted to tear from the experience the same leonine assault on life, but the nature and etiquette of each tournament would never yield it to him.

Something was changing. The knight's frustration was more than just a nostalgia for battle. He had not found what he had set out to achieve through his many conquests. Even if he were to return to the cries of war, it would have made little difference. The knight's appetite could not be sated – and the more he saw it, the more the fight went out of him.

And as these changes unfolded, the horse knew that an important stage of his life was over. It was a strange fate to discover a destiny on the plains of battle only to witness its abrupt end. Could he find another rider? He knew this would never happen; he and his rider were meant for each other.

But something is about to change. I am sure of it.

Late one night, curry-combed and fresh, the horse was drifting between waking thoughts, his head leaning on the ledge of his box. The stables were dark; little light crept through the cracks in the woodwork. He heard shuffling by the door that, without stretching his mind, he took to be a rat. Then he saw the outline of a larger creature, almost entirely hidden in the darkness. It was too small for a horse and too large for a dog or a cat. It moved, just enough to reveal the slender outline of its face and delicate features.

*

Early the following morning, his master took him for a long ride. The horse wasn't clear if they were hunting or travelling. Their path took them into densely forested terrain. When they broached the edge of the woods, the horse thought that he had been there before, but the further they went, the more unfamiliar they became. The wood and its trees were old and unfrequented.

They went deeper into the wood, until they came to a lake. The water was as cold, dark and uninviting as a grave, announced by small clusters of reeds. The rider brought them to a halt at the water's edge. There he waited. They could hear nothing but the sound of the birds. The rider dismounted, walked to the very edge of the lake; he took a few paces into it, muttering some words quietly under his breath. The horse couldn't understand it. They stayed like this, standing in the cheerless company of the pool and the loneliness of the forest.

The horse was sure he had never been in this place before, and the abnormal conduct of his master disquieted him and disturbed the otherwise tightly strung bond of understanding between them. The horse didn't like it and became more restless the longer his rider stood before the remorseless dead eyes of the water.

A cry woke them from their twinned reverie. His master spun on his heel; in a moment he had flung his body onto the horse's back. The horse saw another rider ahead of them. It took no more than a glance to see that the other rider kept his horse for squalid purposes. The creature was layered in mud, badly groomed and tempered to his fashion. The rider was ragged, his face savaged by unkempt hair, and he had a stump where his left ear should have been. The mean-featured figure swung a ball on the end of a chain in his right hand, and before the horse knew it, he and his master were being charged. They stirred to meet the assault and drew his sword.

Quick!

As they neared each other, the opposing rider raised the ball and chain to swing it in circles above his head. The horse was sure, given his master's experience, that the rider who had ambushed them would get more than he had bargained for; but to the horse's – and his master's – surprise, just as the two riders were about to collide, they heard another succession of shouts, this time from the trees on either side of them. The horse kept his head down, but he was aware of people running at them, and he could hear missiles flying. Something like several rocks struck the horse on his haunches, another on his back and another on his front leg. Then he caught the unmistakable whistle of an arrow, as it cut the air. It must have met its target, because he could feel his master wince, and then the trickle of blood around his ribs.

His master struck a parrying blow with his sword as the charging rider brought the ball on his chain down. The ball deviated from its intended path and grazed the horse high on his left front leg. Several stabs of pain punctured his body, and in a loud cry of agony, he stumbled forward, twisting the front portion of his left leg. The horse fell forward. His master turned over the horse's head and landed on his back, a little way forward.

The people who had ambushed his master set about him like wolves. They kicked him, hit him and stabbed him. The horse could feel pain all down his left side that made him feel it was impossible to stand up. He was flattened, with his left front leg tucked under his body, his face grounded in the direction of his unseated lord. He heard feet running and cries above all the commotion. The feet belonged to the man who had been riding the other horse. The man had lost the ball and chain; in its place he carried a lance. The band of bandits cleared a space so that their leader could bring the assault to its natural conclusion. The man with no ear stood over the horse's master and, in a swift and seamless motion, brought the lance down.

Blood choked from the knight's mouth.

*

The assassins wasted no time. They plundered the young knight's body, stealing his weapons, jewellery, and most of his clothes.

A couple of them peeled away and helped the horse up from his trapped position. Pain spiked through him and he exhaled in a short, sharp gasp of air. As they lifted him, he was convinced that he wouldn't be able to stand on his left leg, and he would be forced to hop forward. His captors, for all their brutality, treated him gently and encouraged him to test his strength. When he lowered it to the floor, the pain sharpened, but he knew that it would withstand his weight. He was less sure about how much worse the pain would get after he had been walking for any distance.

The man who had killed his master came over to inspect the horse. He crouched down to examine the wound, then, at little more than a glance, he dismissed it with a wave of his hand. But as the man returned to his full height, he turned his attention to the flesh his weapon had torn. The horse couldn't see the wound, but he knew it was bad. The man muttered something; his companions offered their reply by way of a murmur. They stripped the horse of his finery and at the sound of a shrill and sudden call, the group of bandits took to a march.

The horse caught the sight of his master, now stripped of life and possessions, lying naked under the trees.

Too much had happened in too little time, for him to make sense out it.

Why did he go out to the lake?

He was frightened for his immediate safety; that they had bothered to help him to his feet hardly meant they would keep him safe. What were his captors planning to do with him? Then again the deeper alarm was the loss of his rider. The life his dead master had brought him was everything, as far as the horse was concerned. He could see clearly that without it, and without his knight, he was little more than useless.

And for all the courage and strength his former master had shown, he wondered if he had suffered an ignominious end. Had he really deserved it? Or had his master known what would happen to him? Had he even gone looking for it? Then there were the horse's new companions. What did they want with him? He was badly injured. If he hadn't known this from the pain, he could tell from the faintly troubled way his captors kept their eyes on him.

Behind these thoughts another occurred. Except it was indistinct. It haunted him with the hushed rustle of the wind in the trees, and the chorus of birdsong. It was something he had once known – a memory.

His captors lived within walking distance of the forest. They seemed to treat a ramshackle stone barn as their home. At least, they spent the next few weeks living there, straying only into the fields about them and the edges of the woodland. The group leader – the man who had charged and murdered his master – tended to the horse, grooming him and nursing the wound.

The horse didn't know how to relate to the band of brigands and the man who led them. With his knight they had shared an instinct, and by way of it, a destiny, to a degree that required no thought or judgement. But his new master was aloof – the outward signs of care and attention were not attended with any feeling or compassion. If anything moved the man's mind and body to care for the horse, it was calculation.

The bandits lived in a degree of poverty, and to forestall their complete destitution, they drew on their initiative. The ringleader would disappear for days at a time, with one or two of the others, then return with fresh merchandise or other proceeds of their crimes. Money, food, wine, other livestock – they had no single interest.

The ringleader would look over the horse in passing, mulling on one or more thoughts that he usually discarded as worthless, before he walked off. The only figure who paid more than passing attention to the horse was a young girl, who came to visit him most days, and would take the time to pet him, feed him and examine his injuries. Once or twice, he had noticed her watching him as he frisked about the field. When he caught sight of her, he would stop, then consider the girl, before he walked across to her so that he might take the measure of her business.

As often as not her 'business' was only to watch him, which she did at length and with the same delight. When he came up close to her, she would talk to him, climb onto the fence and rub his nose. Her eyes would stray over his injury.

After a little while of this, an idea must have taken hold in her mind, because she would show up every day (or almost every day) and, cross-legged on the ground, she would set to work with some cloth and what looked like sticks. She was very taken with the activity, borne out by the smile on her face and the evident satisfaction with which she carried it out.

Some days later satisfaction turned to excitement; she hurried up to the horse, caught his attention, and made a great display of showing him the cloth. It was cut in a rectangular shape, like a flag, and she held it between both hands. At first the horse couldn't really make out what was on it. Somehow – with her sticks – she had introduced lines onto the cloth that combined to form the outline of a shape. It took him a few moments to realise that the shape looked something like a horse and that she had therefore contrived to represent his image on the cloth.

He studied his impression. The line was uneven, and the figure it made was only an approximation to his actual shape. But to see the shadow of his being on the cloth was strange. He didn't entirely understand, but the cloth meant that he could see himself – in a sense for the first time – but in a different way. He was both present and absent in the image.

The girl could see the horse's curiosity and it delighted her. She had performed some small trick that drew on the elaborate cadences of nature. The horse, from a little confused and sharing in the joy of his companion, pulled a peculiar face by baring his teeth and snorting. The girl laughed.

The horse didn't know what to make of the girl. She was unlike anyone else he had known.

She means me no harm, I suppose.

But what did she want from him? It was hard to say. All the other people he had known, had approached him with purpose. The girl, on the other hand, had no obvious purpose. She was intrigued by the horse, curious and playful, a disposition to which the horse didn't entirely know how to react.

All the same, the novelty itself tended his curiosity. He found that he looked forward to her visits, that he wanted to study and follow her movement, to anticipate what she might do next. There was something whimsical and unpredictable about the way she behaved, out of keeping with the regimented existence he had kept before. She appealed to him; all the same he knew, with a clarity that equalled his instinct about his former knight, that he would never belong to the girl.

The unlikely transformation of dalliance into sobriety almost always led the horse back to the same thought that began with the same recollection: the stripped body of his former master left to rot before the roof of the dark wood. He had not abandoned his knight; rather the knight had been taken from him. For all that, the accident of these circumstances made a weak appeal to his judgement. The horse belonged with his master, and by following the wayward flight of the brigands, he had betrayed that bond, and betrayed the burning fire that had brought him forth.

The light is you.

So the boy's ghost had said. Was it fading? The horse didn't know how to respond to this feeling, or right the judgement it occasioned. It only left him troubled.

For all that, mutual interest led to other business. Before long, the girl was standing in the company of the horse and the ringleader of the bandits, waving her arms. Her manner was more withdrawn and meeker in the company of the man. When she wasn't gesticulating, she would use her hands to push back her black hair in a way that made her look nervous. Her apparent fear reckoned with the plan she sketched out before him – a plan that turned on the horse. The ringleader's expression was grave, his mind undecided.

However grave and undecided it had been at the time of the girl's entreaties, it was made up soon enough. After a few days, a small ensemble wheeled a waggon, festooned in a simple blue cloth and patched with rough-looking figures, fixed to the material in the same way the girl had fixed the horse's image to the cut of cloth she had waved before him. They draped a similar object over the horse, not unlike a knightly caparison, and harnessed him to the cart. The girl, heavily dressed and wearing a blue crespina, emerged anxiously from the group. Her eyes darted about. The ringleader, whose decision had made all this possible and whose authority instilled fear in those about him, was nowhere to be seen. In fact, almost none of the original band who had ambushed the horse and his knight were present.

A man also dressed in blue and who the horse had never seen before, stood at the horse's side, holding his harness and guiding him in the right direction as he pulled the waggon. The man said almost nothing. For a little while the girl walked at the side of the horse, chattering away to some of those about her.

They walked for an hour or more, before they arrived at a small settlement. Some sort of negotiation took place at the entrance to the village and then the party proceeded, not before the girl disappeared from his side and apparently climbed onto the waggon – the horse could hear the wooden boards creaking and feel a delicate increase in the strain of his burden.

Small groups of people from the settlement came out to meet them once they had assembled in the centre of the village. A few shouts harkened more villagers to their company. The horse could feel and hear the girl (and possibly someone else) prancing about, to the delight of the gathering, who gave out cheers and other plaudits. The horse was curious to see what was taking place, but he also understood what was required of him.

Just at the point the horse thought the entertainment had run its course, a voice broke out. It was the girl's. He was sure of that. Except she was singing. The lyric tumbled out of her and appeared to recount a story that met with bursts of laughter or affected taunts from the crowd. The cheerful song and the pleasure it gave, raised the mood of the horse and made him wish to retain the company of the girl who had given him this role.

Feasts of entertainment like this quickly became his regular business. The small troupe of itinerant entertainers travelled from place to place, village to village, even straying into larger fortified settlements to take stage at extended festivities. Some of these places the horse thought he recognised from his former life as a warrior's mount. How different it was to see them through the spectacle of laughter. People cheered, shouted, sang along, sometimes cried, often elevating their sentiments by drawing on each other.

The mood burgeoned and receded in reaction to

whatever treat was on display. Sometimes the temper turned bawdy; some ladies from the troupe hawked favours to the local men, and the horse noticed that there was always at least someone so taken with drink that they would drift around semi-naked, frightening the children. One such man stole the crowd's attention. He stood naked, except for a ladies wimple, holding an argument with the corpse of a chicken. The crowd laughed at him, and found greater amusement each time the man turned around to bait them for disturbing his rancour.

This was a very different kind of life. The danger, exhilaration, and animal striving he had known with his knight had gone. In its place stood laughter, joy, entertainment, greed, lust and drunkenness. The occasion was always – or almost always – enjoyable. Except in time, he became restless. There wasn't much for him to do. He pulled the waggon and then watched as those about him fell into their revelry. In the end, he thought what he had always known – that he was made for other things.

The girl was pleased with the horse. After their first tour, she came to him in the early evening carrying a bucket of pasture grass. She held him in her gaze for a little while, then pulled from her person the same cloth with his image. She waved it before him, smiling. Then she found a way to fix it to the fence of the makeshift paddock.

The horse watched her wandering away towards a large bonfire and the group that gathered around it. Then he looked again at his image impressed onto the cloth. It flickered in the wind a little, and as the light went out of the day, the shadows tricked him into thinking the representation of his form made subtle movements. The image intrigued and troubled him, and for a reason he couldn't understand, the same memory that had been working to make itself known came to him.

His life with the girl and her troupe of minstrels came to an end much sooner than he had hoped. They had set out one afternoon in the usual fashion, and wound up by early evening in a pitched field heaving with people. (The horse thought he recognised the familiar course of the joust.) Tents, carts, and many other people and animals swirled around the field, competing for attention.

The girl had climbed into the cart and was in the flow of her acrobatics when a disturbance caught the attention of the silent and sullen man whose only function seemed to be to keep watch over the horse. An old woman hurried up to the man, soliciting his attention and asking him for charity. The man tried to brush her away, but when this didn't work, he let go of the horse and pushed the woman forcefully into the crowd. There was a shout, then a curse, before a fight broke out. In the middle of it – the horse didn't know where the blow came from – he felt a sharp stab in his left side, close to the place of his recent wound. He let out a great cry, then thrashed about, before rearing up on his hind legs. By doing so, he overturned the cart, and on coming back into contact with earth, more pain twisted through the front-left flank of his body. Disorder spread about him.

He never pulled the cart back to the encampment, but somehow his company, including the girl, traipsed home, limping most of the way. All of them were downcast, and anger had settled on their silence, but who felt it the greatest and for what reason was hard to say.

The horse was rested for a long time after that and left to his own thoughts. He never saw the girl again, but after his extended absence, the ringleader of the bandits returned to the horse's field, from where he assessed the horse's health, moved only by the same dispassionate act of calculation.

The ringleader meant the horse no harm. His interest was only that of a leader confronted by his next decision. It took time before the nature of the decision became known, but the horse could see that the man had reached it quickly and that it had been dictated by the gravity of the horse's injury. The stabbing had worsened his original affliction.

As the man walked away, the horse noticed that the cloth with his image on it had been removed from his field.

*

The horse was to be sold. The wound at the top of his left leg was recovering, but something about it wouldn't heal entirely. He would wince as he circuited the field; and the stubbornness and persistence of his trauma was evident to the thieves.

In the end, he was sold, not for his agility but for the only quality that remained – his power. He was sold into a life of labour.

The exchange took place on the edge of a small settlement. The horse thought he recognised it, and even thought it looked a little like the city that had been the objective of his first battle; but the now-familiar keep that still haunted his mind was nowhere in sight.

He was taken into a yard tucked uncomfortably amidst a hustle of buildings, and presented to a barrel-chested man who could never settle the impatience of his business and regarded the horse and his vendor with professional disdain. After a distracted survey, which paid undue attention to the horse's injury, the two men discussed terms of sale, until the portly man beckoned to one of his labourers, and the horse was ushered away into a new stable.

If the horse met the bandit's coldness with indifference, he hated everything about his new home. His new owner – who seemed to run the complex of buildings – was marked by malice but kept it under control for the sake of his livelihood. It surfaced in harsh words and brutal body blows to those about him, including the horse. This streak of violence never disappeared – it was there, visible as an intemperate glint in his eyes, which was enough to check the behaviour of his workers.

A hapless young boy was the most frequent victim. At his gentlest, the owner would smack the back of the boy's head; more frequently, he would kick him from behind, sometimes pushing him over with the sole of his foot, and at other times he would punch the mite, almost square in the face. The horse couldn't know the boy's offence, but there was more than punishment in the brutality of the blows – the portly man dealt them out with cruelty and a dark layer of pleasure.

This casual care for violence had become almost a custom. The horse learned quickly to expect beatings and blows as a spur to action and greater effort. Given the monotony and grind of his work, the pain that came from the routine strikes and whippings was one of the few things that rekindled the life in his body. Was this the point? Did it teach him to discover deeper reserves of effort, until all his strength was spent?

'Meat! That's what they'll use you for – meat!'

This was the opinion of the only other horse who shared his labour.

'That's what happened to the last one. He gave out and they chopped him up. Then they were roasting him on the spit. Sooner you than me! Sooner you than me!'

The two horses worked in a round and cramped building, where they were tethered to a contraption at its centre and made to walk in circles. The weight of turning the contraption was, with one or two rotations, nothing to stretch any horse's endurance, but hour after hour, its weight grew steadily, as if it were dragging each animal in a dark, dead pool devoid of all movement.

'It's called a mill,' said his companion one night, but made little more of the name.

The horse found everything about the work stifling. The physical space of the buildings (including the stable) was much more squashed than anything he had ever known. Every room squeezed out the air, leaving barely enough for his body to inhale. Tied to the contraption and bound to an interminable life of repetitions, the horse could also feel the impact on his body. Every part of him wanted to break against the narrow boundaries all about him. His muscles flexed, his breath sought to quicken; he wanted to run and kick forward. It maddened him, as wave after wave of power surged inside him, but couldn't be directed in the way his body had come to expect. Instead, his muscles soaked up the power in a different way – with it, he could feel his body (and mind) contorting to fit the suffocating possibilities of this existence.

'New to this, aren't you?' said his companion.

'Yes,' muttered the horse.

'Think you're somewhere else, I'll bet. I can tell – the way you pull. You don't pull it steady.'

'Sorry.'

'Not to worry, they'll break you.'

*

His new masters needn't have used any other tactics, as the horse could feel himself bending slowly, or shrinking as it felt to him, to fit his new routine. Nevertheless, they went to work on him, and tried as best they could to instil new fears. They shocked him with noises. One of the men, at the end of the day, would sometimes surprise him by shaking an object close to one of his ears. The noise was cutting, deafening and unbearable. It made him spook, whinny, sometimes scream. The first few times they did it, he heard his companion laughing, as soon as the noise died down and his tormentor left the stable.

The more time the horse had spent with the knight, the more he had directed all his energy into the purpose of their conquests. So much so that he had spent less of his own time thinking; instead he had only anticipated the next ride. He had surrendered his body, all his thoughts and memories, to his former master.

In this new incarcerated life, things were different. The natural range of his instinct was blocked at every turn. While he could feel his body 'breaking', his mind would wander, especially at night. Without a target on which to set his sights, his thoughts retreated into reflection.

All the labourers, he sensed, performed their duties more from a sense of fear than any other emotion. Even the owner, the brute who instilled fear in them all, lived not for love, but had made a pact with some other purpose. Why did any of them do it? If they were all coerced, where did this begin, with whom and why?

In the pattern of his thoughts, he could see his temperament at work. This sort of reflection came from a frustrated drive to live as he had once done, and that he couldn't, made him want to understand why. Even if he wasn't always aware of it, he was striving for his former chivalrous life.

But now, you see, I don't deserve it. I forfeited that life.

Guilt weighed on the horse's mind. He knew that he should have left with his knight; the two of them should have perished in the same charge. They were meant to live and die fighting together. The horse had the vaguest memories now of the time before his life on the battlefield; he saw himself back then as an undirected force, a spirit trying to find a form that suited the appetites of his body. His knight had provided the direction and given him the form he had been seeking. Except now that his knight was dead, his situation had changed again. His breath of life was not undirected; rather it was trapped, shackled to the form of the mill and its grain-counting fist of order.

Is this the price I am meant to pay? By surviving, is this my punishment?

Had he hesitated, even for just a moment, when he saw that his master was in trouble? Had he been too startled by the sight of the bandits bearing down on the defeated rider? Should he have done something?

Until now, the horse had been prepared to tender his will to his human masters. It had never felt to him that he was merely a dull instrument in their short-sighted schemes; he had felt more like a torch and they were the torchbearers. With his knight their shared light had burnished to a white flame. Except now things had changed; now, his human masters had erected a carefully constructed boundary around him, and inside the torch he carried was turning a plangent shade of old age.

It seemed to the horse that, as these thoughts returned in shifting spectres of the same substance, he was faced with a choice: either he could accept the enclosing walls and tightening air that would put him to rest, or he could rebel against his captivity.

Usually, as he reached the small hours, his mind would take another turn. He found that as he drifted in and out of half-sleep, images came to him – and they were often the same images. He saw a quiet valley, a simple track, hugged by the soft outline of the hills. He couldn't see himself, but he could hear his hooves trotting forward on the broken floor. Ahead, there was a building. Then, at other times, he saw a bird – an unusual white-breasted creature. It flew ahead of him, just treading the currents of air along a mountain ridge.

These images were different from his reflections. His thoughts about his new labour were propelled by animal aggression. The images came to him when he was scarcely awake. They occurred when he had let all his other thoughts drift.

He knew that they were more than surface images. They were records of something or somewhere he had once known. They were memories. More than that, he was sure that they were calling him – calling him back. He couldn't give them more detail, but he felt sure that they were united by a single place.

When he had the chance, sometimes in the drudgery of his daily routine, he mulled over these late-night recollections. He had not sought them out; they had found him, and only once his jaded mind and body had relinquished their own temporary designs. They were the thoughts of a meandering, wandering, lost mind; and yet they made him curious. What was this place he had once known? Where was it? Why was it home? And why, despite the last pass at a vocation that suited the power and passion of his body, did he want to return to it?

Such thoughts, and others like them, became something like an obsession; they haunted him the more he indulged them, to the point where he became convinced that this place, this 'home' he could remember, was the only place he truly belonged.

His deliberating drift towards a final sortie and his fascination with the unformed memories that came to him in the night dovetailed slowly, trodden out after weeks of labour. One would lead to the other, he thought. On the far side of his last clarion call, he was sure that he would be able to call to mind clearly these vestiges that had once held some meaning for him.

Then that's what I should do. And somehow I must find a way to do it.

But, on the back of his resolve, he couldn't put his thoughts to a good pursuit. Rather, a kind of lassitude set in. He subsisted in an unhappy relationship with his work and the gloomy industry of the mill. He couldn't find the fire in his belly. Had his spirit withdrawn to the ethereal reflections that sustained him through the night? Was he just too weary of the world?

Then, one afternoon the mill owner made an uncharacteristic appearance as the two horses were lost in the hypnotic cycle of their business; uncharacteristic because the mill owner always delegated supervision of the two horses to a miller. A shout introduced his entrance and he was preceded by another man, a figure who the horse had not seen before. The latter wore a scuffed leather waistcoat, patched with dirt and grime. His skin was tan, and a nascent beard cast a shadow over his face. He pointed, indignant in his animation, at a noticeable hole proximate to one of the main arterial beams supporting the roof. The forceful and defensive manner of his conduct suggested he was engaged in an argument over a matter of business.

The mill owner was moved only to shrug his shoulders and offer begrudging one-word replies, until the debate discovered more heat. The mill owner pulled a rondel dagger from his clothing and slammed it into the beam. The other man stepped back into silence. In predatory pursuit, the mill owner reached out to grab the man by the neck. Everyone in the mill, including the two horses, stopped to watch. The stranger started to struggle and choke a little, and without knowing why exactly, the horse was engulfed by such a wave of anger that he whinnied and made a futile attempt to rise up, pulling so hard that the mill's axle shook.

The mill owner, obviously disturbed by the horse's interruption, kept his eyes on the other man, but gave him back his windpipe. In response the stranger knocked the dagger sticking out of the wall to the floor and stormed out of the building. Its owner stood, contemplating the fracas for a time. Then he turned to stare at the horse. What was in his mind, the horse couldn't say, but the long and lingering look spoiled with competition.

In the short term, nothing more came of the episode, but in a curious way, the horse was encouraged by his reaction. All his thoughts and reflections had settled for a fight, and the anger was so great that he would have gladly brought the whole building down in the struggle. He knew nothing about the stranger or the bad business with the mill owner, but his hatred for his new owner turned his mood molten.

A few days later, the horse was being led through the courtyard back to the stables for the evening, when he saw another stranger on the near side of the gate. It wasn't uncommon to see strangers wandering around the complex of buildings; they were a natural part of its commerce and congress. The figure stood out in part because his dress was unusual, and in part because the horse thought he recognised him. The horse had come to learn that men who wore this attire were called monks. He wore a simple black robe with a cincture and a hood, and had tonsured grey hair with a beard as withering and hoary as the rest of his emaciated frame.

He also stood in relief because he was staring intently at the horse. The horse wondered why, but then he realised that he recognised the monk. He didn't know from where, but he was certain their paths had crossed, possibly more than once. The horse had seen monks on his many warring adventures, and they would often appear at the fortress he and his old master had besieged in their first fight, so he assumed that this figure fell into place somewhere in the intervals of this time. And yet, he couldn't give their meeting a location.

The monk walked across the courtyard to catch the attention of the miller who was leading the horse by the rein; they met in a jovial fashion, and the monk approached as if to admire the horse's physical finery, but the shifting business of his eyes betrayed his true intention. The monk knew the horse, just as the horse knew the monk.

The horse thought the monk might have known more about the horse than the horse could return; still, he rejected the notion that what he had so stubbornly forgotten would yield to a clear memory. The monk, he thought, was the shadow of a creature he had once known. The person standing before him was real enough. The cassock, the tonsure, the cut-glass face, high forehead, and frosted beard were plain and particular to his sight; but the particulars would not reveal his true self, which lay hidden, only suggested by these subtleties and refinements of flesh. If it made any sense to think of it in such terms, it was this hidden face of the monk's being that the horse had known. The monk, so the horse wanted to believe, looked back with the same dull recognition.

The elusive nature of these thoughts was only compounded when the monk ran his hand over the horse's nose and neck. The act of touching excited the sense that the monk's face was in fact a shadow cast by the person it concealed.

The monk's hand left the body of the horse as his eyes fell on the signs of the horse's injury. This too had some meaning. The horse looked at the monk; and after a moment of carefully studying the wound, the monk brought his eyes back to meet the horse's.

The moment ended. The monk shook the miller's hand, and they went about their business.

In the closed space of his stable, his mind fused the monk's appearance with the stirring memories that had come to occupy him. He couldn't shake the image of the holy man, so certain was he that they had met before, albeit not in quite the same way. The horse didn't know what was at work, but he felt haunted, tracked by the near presence of something. As the night wore on, the horse even came to think that the monk, deliberately or otherwise, had appeared so that he might shift the horse's compass entirely.

If, as he thought, the outward presentation of the monk only partially exposed his true character, it didn't take the horse long to apply the same thought to himself; in other words, was he only partially present in the eyes of those about him, and were the persistent memories, the echo or trace of something more? And with it, he began to think about his experiences on the plain, as a workhorse, as a partner in the troupe of minstrels, and most of all, as a steed of war; each episode, in retrospect, unfolded in no more than a flick of his tail. They came as quickly as they went, in which case was each beginning and end the shadow that obscured its source?

All of which confirmed that, really, he was not trying to return to his former life of nobility and honour; the light that had brought him forth, clearly outshone him, bleeding around his edges. The arc of any one act was insufficient to contain it. In which case his 'return' would not take him back to the chivalrous manners of the battlefield, but instead away from the plain on a search for the places, images and memories that eluded him.

Several nights later a lantern appeared at the entrance to the stable. It hovered by the doorway, casting a dim light over the character who held it aloft. Then the figure opened the hatch and came close enough to reveal his face; the horse saw that it was the mill owner, a fold of tension visible on his forehead, even in the soft candlelight.

The mill owner brought the horse out of the stable, and guided only by the light of the lantern, led him to the mill. There he fixed the torch on a stake, so that it threw its weak light about the circular room, and tethered the horse to the mill. The horse's partner was nowhere in sight, and he had no idea other than a foggy sense of foreboding about what was in his owner's mind. Then he noticed, hidden in a corner piled with hay and bundled up on the ground like a spilled sack of grain, the young boy who had so often met the mill owner's ire.

Once the horse was fastened to his daily burden, the owner slapped his haunches to signal that work should begin. The horse began to pull. On his first rotation, he saw his owner grinning at him. It was a smile as sharp as the dagger with which he had violated the building and offered with as much good humour. The horse continued on his circuit, but two thirds of the way round, he heard a yelp, a high-pitched, piteous plea, followed by some shuffling about. With a little more urgency, the horse returned to find the mill owner pulling hard on a tuft of hair at the back of the boy's head as the boy writhed, squirmed and cast about in blind pain and anguish. The horse, disturbed by this latest turn, continued to pull, but harder and quicker.

On the next rotation, he heard a cry, followed quickly by another, then a brittle crack and a scream. By the time he emerged in sight of the scene of crime, the young boy had a limp arm and a face streaming with blood. The horse stopped, his anger tearing, pulsing, bursting. He was about to strain at his halter, when the mill owner turned on him, fists raised ready to pummel and a maniacal mist of choler in his eyes, then shouted a demand that required no literal comprehension to know that the horse should keep pulling or else. The horse, involuntarily and more than a little frightened, obeyed.

More cries, screams, shuffling and the heavy breathing of assault, accompanied his next pointless circuit, and he returned to find the boy kneeling forward. An unnatural cascade of blood had replaced the boy's face, and his body swayed towards the edge of consciousness. The mill owner grabbed the boy by his ripped tunic and broke his jaw with another pulping blow. The horse reached the limit of what he was prepared to endure, and he strained so hard at his halter that a creak broke through the lambent light and made the lantern flicker.

The mill owner again turned on the horse, rising up to him, bearing his fists, shouting and invoking every curse his hellish tongue could summon. The owner cast about, evidently looking for a weapon of some description or even a stick or pipe, anything he might use to discipline and subdue the horse once and for all. The horse strained again. This time the creak became a crack, but in which part of his intricate incarceration the horse couldn't tell. Even so, he could feel something give, granting him the smallest gasp of freedom, but enough to rally every last crystallised beat of anger in his body to destroy his futile collar, this futile mill and the malfeasance of its order. The life, the light, was there before him, calling him on so that he could almost feel it all about him, and nothing, no mechanical act of will, would blight his path.

With a crepitating snap that made the whole building lurch, the horse came to his freedom, and he reared up at the mill owner. The owner turned back on the recalcitrant creature, but found the horse at full height. The horse's right hoof landed on the owner's chest and pinioned him to the ground, smashing the breath beneath it.

The horse didn't wait. He ran out of the barn, across the courtyard, out of the gate, and into the street beyond.

The Return

The horse didn't linger long – his blood quickened and he came to life. He had spent the night wandering at a trot through empty streets. No-one was awake and no lights burned in any of the buildings. Cats coiled their limbs in dark corners, and rats swept the streets clean. By way of the main road, he had come to the edge of the settlement. A dirt track led him forward and struck out in an empty expanse of uncultivated land. He sniffed the air, sensing a way forward.

A bridge led the way beyond the buildings. It rose over a river that skirted the edges of the settlement. The water was wide, and the community had obviously gone to some trouble in crossing it, which marked out the construction as an important – perhaps the most important – point of access. The horse walked up to the bridge, his hooves rattling the wooden boards. He had no mind to do anything other than walk, but a noise came to him two-thirds of the way over. It sounded like the movement of something either entering or leaving the flow of the river.

The horse stopped, listened for a little while, hoping the noise might reveal more of itself, but nothing came. If his walk across the bridge had disturbed something, perhaps it was now waiting for him to leave? Unless, of course, it was preparing an ambush. But something told the horse that there were no creatures nearby.

He approached the side of the bridge and looked over the edge, down into the running water. It was still too dark to make out the features of everything without his mind playing tricks; but he could see the water clearly enough and the way it rustled over the rocky bed. Light borne from somewhere undetectable would catch ripples, betraying its presence if not its full character. The horse looked again. He thought he could see something, but it was impossible to know what. He went closer.

He hurried over the rest of the bridge and found his way onto the riverbank, sinking down carefully until his front legs were at the water's edge. The darkness was all about him, which still made it hard to make out what, if anything, he had heard; but the closer he came, the more he thought he could detect an outline. He lowered his head. Then, broken by the rippling surface and the faint light, he saw a face – the face of a horse.

It was talking; at least, its mouth gave that impression, but nothing audible reached him. As far as he possibly could, the horse drew closer still, so that his nose almost pierced the dark gloss on the surface of the river. There, he heard something – or thought he did. The sound, as best he could make out, was a voice, but the substance of its speech was still impossible to hear. The voice was sunk, a drowned and watery whisper. And yet for all the impediments to its cause, the face of the horse would not give up – it talked and talked, until by chance a fleeting hiatus in the chorus around it allowed two words to escape:

'... black hills ...'

No sooner had these words taken flight, than the loophole through which they had found freedom closed. The horse was about to speak. *What did you say?* was what he wanted to utter, but the futility of the effort checked his initiative; and besides, the face of the horse had gone.

For the briefest moment, the scene returned to its natural elements. The water flowed over the river-bed, until another event troubled him. First he heard – or thought he heard – something jump and fall back on itself in the water. It came from under the bridge again. He stared into the darkness. It was too pitch to penetrate, until he caught a glimmer of something gliding along. It followed the short distance from the bridge and became more visible as it got closer to him, as if it were rising from the bed of the river.

His vision, however hampered by the poor light, told him that it was a light or a flame, much like the one he had seen in a river before. The flame came closer to the surface and closer to him; it slowed down, stopping to tread against the current.

He watched the light. It appeared to hover beneath the surface, suggesting that it had charted a course towards him and was now soliciting a response. The horse waited, expecting something to happen. His head twitched a little.

He started to lower his head, so that he might examine the light; but he had scarcely moved when the flame burst through the water in a blaze. The horse was shocked by the sudden breach of peace, but also blinded. Set against the dark, it erupted in a display of brilliant brightness. He lurched backwards, treading uneasily on the upward slope of the riverbank.

Then, before he had any chance to compose himself or adjust his vision, he was attacked. He could feel it approach and burn him, right at the point of his wound. The edge of his coat smarted at the pain, and for a terrifying moment, he thought he would catch fire. He let out a loud cry.

But the pain he could feel soon changed. It smuggled a way beneath his hide, into his body. The light was seeking a way to enter him, and had found a route through his wound. He could feel – a sensation unlike anything he had experienced before – the fire penetrate him slowly. When he tried to look down to catch some sight of his assailant, it had gone.

In something like a panic, he ran up the bank of the river, then circled and staggered about, as if his movements might exorcise the thing that had just entered him. Pain lingered at the site of his wound, but not behind it. In fact he could no longer locate the flame at a single point, even if he knew it was still inside him. It seemed to the horse that his body had absorbed the flame and that every part of him could feel it. Except now it conferred a warm glow of renewed vigour.

He continued to move fitfully, as if expecting to respond to an external object, and as his body caught up with the idea that there was nothing to which he could respond, he became steadier and more settled. The pain had almost gone, but diffuse and partial traces of it could be felt. He moved as if unsure of each movement, eking out each event of his being with caution.

The black night had started to turn to grey morning, but no single source of light was yet visible. The horse had no real notion of what had just happened, but whatever it was effected a change in him.

He could scarcely sit still; the fire that now stirred and spoiled in the courses and corridors of his body, also looked for an answer in the outside world, as if whatever had invaded him was seeking unity with a source. It moved him and made him restless, but towards what goal or objective he couldn't see.

Now that the river had brought forth its secret, nothing else disturbed the morning quiet. The water returned to its meditative rustle, little or no wind disturbed the air, and no animals or creatures broke the stillness. Only isolated bursts of birdsong called out at the vanguard of the morning. The way this strange event made the horse feel, clashed with the day's peaceful beginning.

Then the light came. He could feel it before he saw it. A faint glow of warmth spread over his head, lifting him out of the shade. Without moving, he raised his eyes to follow the change back to its source. The light spilled over the rippling line of hills in the distance, radiating in a large flare through the gaps and obscuring any distinguishing landmarks in a silhouette.

The black hills.

The voice, sunk and sodden, echoed in his mind, but more than any literal connection, his body was compelled by the morning light. The thing that had entered him wanted to find a home in those streams of sunshine and drew him towards the hills.

He didn't need to ponder the matter any further.

It only remained for him to calculate the best way he could get there. He could see the mountains clear enough, but was it as simple as walking over the land that separated them? A first glance made this sort of simple plan tempting, but he knew enough about the topography of the plain to think again. His time as a knight's mount had taught him that the land was not so accessible that it could just be traversed so freely, and he also knew to expect pitfalls, traps, distractions and the machinations of animal interest. He needed a route, one that would guide him towards his destination.

It was clear to him that the river came from the hills, and the water that found its origin in them, had carried their message. Now that he studied it, the river, as far as he could see from his vantage point, appeared to meander from the mountains. The properties and character of water also told him that the river would lead back to a clear route into the hills. Water was always sure to find valleys, gulleys and crevices that would provide easier opportunities for his final ascent. So, he decided that this was the surest way of return.

He set out along the riverbank, following the opposite direction of the water's current.

*

The countryside was empty. The common land spread out all around. As the sun neared its zenith, he saw a single figure to his left, on the far side of the river, standing upright in the distance. From the way the figure was standing, the horse had the feeling he was being watched, but it was impossible to know for sure. It made little difference to the horse's focus, and flickered only temporarily at the periphery of his thoughts.

The river ran more or less straight for many miles, but by the middle of the afternoon, he could see clearly that it was taking him in a long crescent to the right. It was still a long way off but it looked like the river emerged through a wide gap between two dark eruptions in the land. The hills to the right drifted into the long distance, but were gentler; whereas to the left – those that stood before him – loomed as large black shadows over the plain.

He was examining the water to see if it was safe enough to wade or swim across, when the movement of a creature crept across the corner of his eyes. It was hunched and bobbled forward, partly obscured by the long grasses. The horse stopped. He could see it shuffling along, with something like a limp. It was bent over, revealing only the arch of its back, but he could see just enough to know that it was a human, albeit one with an unusual or damaged gait. It was walking along at twice the width of the river on his right side, but moving diagonally, so that if the two of them were to stay on the same course, they would meet. This, the horse suspected, was deliberate.

At this range, the horse couldn't intuit any danger, but his experience had taught him to be careful. He waited. The human continued with his unsightly limp, and was surely not trying to conceal himself, because the strange manner of his bearing was so conspicuous.

The figure emerged on the bank of the river a little way ahead. He was a man, his spine crooked, but he managed to straighten a little so that he might look at the horse. The man shifted a thought in his mind, then went rummaging for something in the threadbare patchwork of clothing that concealed his body. Brandishing whatever he had found about his person, the man moved towards the horse with the same limp.

It was an apple. The hunched figure held it aloft. From most people, the horse could intuit something about them, but in this case, he felt nothing and couldn't see why. Then again, hunger had never stopped the horse from accepting charity before, even from people he knew were no good.

The horse took a few careful steps forward, then took the apple. The man smiled, then guffawed, before twirling on one foot with a sort of hop and a jig. Words followed, whispered with the same dance of delight; they ushered the horse to business. The horse took no decision to follow and took no decision not to, but found that he was walking along behind the man, apparently indifferent to wherever his will stood on the matter.

The man led the horse away from the river, along a ditch used to drain the land, until they came to a small field of dried earth and stones. A lonely ash tree withered in one corner. A donkey was tied to the tree.

The man surfaced two more apples: one for the horse, the other for the donkey. The horse, almost encouraged by the cheerful appearance of the man, ate the second apple gladly. He only noticed that, like the donkey, he was tied to the tree as the last of the apple slipped down his throat. The man had draped an old piece of rope around the horse's neck; the other end he had knotted to one of the tree's sinewy branches.

The man sat on an upturned bucket on the far side of the tree. From there he busied himself, by shaving or sharpening a piece of wood. He would glance at the horse and the donkey from time to time. Still the horse didn't know what to make of the hunchback.

'Where did you come from?' The donkey muttered in a distracted sort of way.

The horse was about to give one answer before he decided on another.

'Those hills on the horizon.'

'You're a fell pony, then?'

'Something like that,' said the horse.

They watched the man.

'Where do you come from?'

'A farm. Not far from here.'

'Does he work for the farm? The man with the apples, I mean.'

'No,' said the donkey. 'I've never seen him before. He came into my field yesterday afternoon. That was the first time I laid eyes on him.'

'He's a strange fellow,' said the horse.

'Yes,' said the donkey.

The donkey and the horse said very little to each other after that. Neither of them knew why they had been brought together and with little knowledge of their circumstances, they found little to say. The man with the apples pottered about the field, sometimes mumbling to himself. He brought the horse and the donkey some dried grass, as the afternoon dimmed into dusk.

The man lit a fire just behind the two horses, so that neither of them could see it directly, but they caught the playful shadows it created all about them. Something about the position of the fire, the strange behaviour of the man with the apples and the onset of night, troubled the horse and made him fearful.

'You are frightened?' said the donkey.

'A little,' confessed the horse.

'Yes.'

They watched the shadows lurch about them.

'The mountains,' mumbled the donkey.

The horse thought he could hear the man stand up and walk away from the fire, back over the tracks they had followed from the river. The horse sidled around a little, so he could just about look behind him. Sure enough, the man was no longer sitting near the fire, but the horse couldn't see far enough into the night to know his whereabouts.

The night wore on. The horse began to drift into half-sleep, his body tethered to the tree, but his mind only half-tethered to his circumstance. An image of moorland came to him. Then he was awake and alert. Something was near. Something was approaching.

It was a woman, an old woman, marked out by a long white shawl. She walked out of the darkness on the other side of the tree to stand before them. She hugged the shawl tightly around her, so that it arched her shoulders and made her look older and more stooped than perhaps she was. Her hair was brown and tied back, her face roughened by exposure. At their centre, her eyes were black – blacker than the night all about them.

She walked slowly but calmly up to the horse

and the donkey, staring directly at the horse. The horse glanced around at the donkey, but he gave the impression that he hadn't seen the woman.

'What are you doing here, horse?' asked the woman.

An owl called out in the distance.

The horse had never met a human he could talk to before.

'I followed the man with the apples,' replied the horse. 'He fed me. I was hungry and he fed me.'

'And where were you going?'

She stood just under the tree's branch, huddled up but close to the horse's face.

'To the mountains,' said the horse.

'The mountains?' asked the woman.

'Yes.'

The woman reached around to whisper in his ear.

'You've been there before, I suppose.'

She leaned back to her former position.

'I believe so.'

'But you aren't sure?'

'No, I'm not sure.'

The woman thought about the horse's answer.

'Why do you want to go back to the mountains?'

The horse searched his mind. He wanted to give several answers: because they haunted his memory; because he wanted to piece together all the images he could recollect; because he believed they were his true home.

In the end he replied simply:

'Because they are quiet and beautiful.'

Again, the woman mulled over the horse's answer.

'You don't have anything to keep you here? You are not tendered to anyone?'

Technically, the horse had run away, but he refused to believe that anything in his life of servility at the mill and its daily round of labour, amounted to an obligation.

'No,' he said.

'Then what about opportunities? Surely, you must have some of those? You are a fine animal and a powerful creature – surely, there must be a part you could play?'

'I have done my part. I rode with a master for a time.'

'What has become of your master?'

'He has gone to shade.'

'A pity.'

'Yes.'

'But you remain?'

'I'm little use without him.'

'So, this is why you want to return to the mountains?'

The horse turned his head again to see if the donkey was listening, but his position hadn't changed. The donkey, it seemed, could neither see nor hear the woman.

'Yes, that's why I want to return.'

'Then why did you follow this man here? Why did you eat his apples? You had a course but you didn't follow it.'

'I am just … resting.'

'No,' said the woman sternly. 'No, you are not resting.'

'Then what am I doing?'

'You are trapped. This man – this man with the apples – has caught you and trapped you here.'

'Trapped?'

'You are in danger. He is a devil.'

The horse looked over his shoulder towards the fire. Still he could see no sign of the man.

The woman crouched down before him. From within her shawl, she produced a large stone. She reached forward and placed the stone before the horse's forelegs. Then she stood up and reached around again to whisper into the horse's ear.

'If you want to reach the mountains, you cannot hesitate and will never be able to turn back. Once you are there, you will stay there.'

The woman looked into the horse's eyes one more

time.

*

The horse woke in pain. It surged down the whole of his front-left side and originated from the site of his old wound. He blinked and whinnied, then caught the shuffle of feet about him. He flung his head around. Someone was assaulting him. Dawn couldn't have been far away. A grey light helped the landscape emerge from the night, but the sun had not yet spilled over the horizon. The fire still flickered behind him.

Then, worse than any pain, he saw the donkey next to him. The poor creature was tethered to the tree. In fact, its bonds had been strengthened and tightened, so that it scarcely had any room to move. And yet room for manoeuvre was immaterial; its body had been beaten, bludgeoned and struck with a knife – large incursions into its flesh were the source of drying streams of blood. Its life had departed. Its head had been hacked more than halfway off, and hung from its neck, like a grotesque fruit.

The horse caught another strike of pain, this time on the lower flank of his right, hind leg. He staggered around to meet the face of the man with the apples, who cackled and held at his side a long knife burnished with blood.

The horse tried to rear up at the man, but realised quickly that he couldn't move his forelegs. The noose about his neck had been tightened, and when he just managed to peer down, he could see that his front legs had been tied together.

The man with the apples laughed again, and slashed at the horse's right foreleg. Panic and pain burst through the horse. His mind and body wanted to fight, to run, to charge, to struggle for life, but they were bound. And his imprisonment had a clear purpose – the hobbled and hideous man who was laughing before him wanted to tear up his flesh, to flay it and destroy it.

The horse pulled on his noose. The branch bent but stayed fixed firmly to its trunk. His torturer continued a circular study of the horse and catching sight of the old wound on the horse's left foreleg he had just opened up, he jabbed at it again with his knife. The horse sang out in pain, raising his head in the agony, then letting it fall before him. In this helpless position, the horse saw the stone that the woman had placed between his legs.

By shuffling about, he managed to knock it over. He saw that, on its underside, it had a sharp, serrated edge. In this moment of panic, he could see what she had intended. He tried, as best he could, to work the rope that tied his forelegs together, over the serrated edge.

Another sharp incision from the man's blade brutalised his haunches. The horse watched as the man continued to sidle around, so that he stood to the horse's rear. The horse, instinctively and with little or no apparent thought, just managed to balance on his front legs, and kicked out with his back legs as violently as the remaining strength in his body would allow. He met his target. The man went flying and stumbling backwards with such force that he fell and landed in the embers of the fire. There, he howled and scrambled about.

The horse, meanwhile, persevered in breaking his bonds, until the rope frayed. This left the noose about his neck. He pulled on it. The branch stretched to an unnatural degree and started to creak. The end of the rope tied to the branch began to slide along; the horse wasn't sure if the branch or rope would snap first.

By this time his tormentor had climbed out of the fire, but several among his assorted layers of clothing were aflame. The man flung himself on the hard ground and rolled over it, uttering a high-pitched screech in his desperation.

Something broke and the horse staggered backwards. Turning back to the tree, he could see that the branch-end of the rope had come free, catapulting the branch back into its natural shape. The horse danced about on his hooves, not sure what might happen next and testing the limits of his freedom. Pain still tortured many parts of his body, but as soon as he knew he was free, he ran back towards the river, paying no mind to the figure behind him, who was still struggling to stay the fire from his flesh.

*

The horse found the river. From there he ran along its banks, following its subtle twists and turns. The cold grey morning touched everything about him. The first trills of birdsong and stirrings of animal life came slowly. But there was nothing slow and rhythmical about his activity. *Get to the hills and get there as quickly as possible* – that was his one thought. Nothing would stand in his way – day or night, animal, human, weather or the passing obstacles of the landscape. If his body gave out, he would die, but his spirit would continue – one way or another, he would reach his destination.

In the end, the dawn came, relieving the plain from the remaining shivers of night and persuading different forms of life from the shadows. All were alarmed by the sight of the crazed horse running for the hills. A snake coiled across the sandy dunes towards the river; ducks took flight from the cover of reeds, alarmed by the heavy drumbeat of the horse's gallop; and a wild boar ran away in panic. An hour or more later, the horse almost trampled a woman, who emerged from a cluster of bushes by the river, carrying a basket. She screamed. The horse reared up on his hind legs, but even this passing fright did nothing to impede his purpose. He took off with the same delirium.

The horse ran for most of the morning. The river, despite its indecisive meanders, was clearly heading towards a gap in the hills, taking a long, slow drift to the right. To reach the line of black hills, he would have to cross the river. The horse could see the gap getting nearer, so that he could just make out features of the landscape, but he had no way of knowing whether it would be easier to cross the river now or later.

With no care to deliberate, he found an easy route down to the water and waded out. In a little while, he was just out of his depth, being dragged gently by the current back in the direction from which he had come. He kicked, struggled and urged his body forward with every excitable part of him, until his legs connected with the sludgy sediment on the far shore. He clambered up the bank, and continued to run along the left bank of the river.

Throughout his long run, he saw almost no-one. Apart from the woman he had frightened, he was watched from a distance by a farmer, and two women washing some garments on the other side of the river stood to catch the sight of him going by. The pain seemed to fade away the more he exerted his limbs, but as his journey wore on, it returned, not as the sharp invasions with which it had been given, but as great pulses dragging his body to the earth.

He wouldn't give in to it, any more than he would have yielded to any creature that tried to halt him; but there was only so much hard running he could manage, and as he followed the course of the river into the gap in the hills, he was forced to slow his pace.

A little way beyond the gap, he could see the land rise sharply, climbing up to the ridge he had been pursuing all day. The ascent was too steep to climb, but a track climbed up behind it and disappeared into what looked like a narrow valley. The horse, sure only of his intention, followed the track at a trot. He hoped it would curl around the back of the ridge and provide an easier pathway into the hills.

As he reached the rise at the head of the valley, he could feel something give way around the knee of his left foreleg. He staggered about, breathing heavily, as if assaulted and struggling to stay on all fours. He stopped. His heart hammered. His vision was partly blurred, and he thought he could hear something, beyond the chirrup of birds and the sibilant breath of the wind in the tall grasses. It was a long, low echoing tune, nothing like the cry or call of any animal he had ever heard – and yet he was convinced it was a call.

From his position, he could see for miles down the valley. Trees grew in patches along its lower parts on either side, rising up to a neat line where they gave way to moorland. They hugged the gentle trail of a small stream, paralleled on one side by the track he had found.

He knew this place. It was more beautiful than he had imagined or could remember. If the sound he had heard was anything, he liked to think it was the call of the valley. To his left, and as he had expected, a grassy path climbed up over the common and swung around onto a summit, then down along the ridge. This was the obvious route to follow and as he looked down the valley, he thought he could detect two things: first, he heard the same sound calling to him (more distant and ethereal this time); second, he could see a building, compressed to a miniature and placed at a small bend in the long arc of the valley's shape.

The horse, at a slow trot and limping badly, followed the call.

The journey down the valley was long and laborious. He couldn't find a pace greater than his afflicted walk, and a combination of the exhaustion and his swelling pustules of pain, meant that he had begun to lose feeling and all sensibility of his surroundings. It felt to him that he was leaving pieces of himself in a trail down the track. For all the pain and disorientation, his every step returned him to something familiar, which made him keep going, as if he had only partially penetrated the fold of the land and its unusual charms.

Flies flew about him. A squirrel scaled the trunk of a tree and a pigeon took flight noisily from the tree-tops. His breathing grew worse; from laboured rasping, it turned into moments of coughing. He blinked. The valley blurred and then came back into focus. A little way ahead he could see the building. He knew it now, though he had only ever seen it before from the ridge.

He also knew who lived there: the small community of monks he could see milling around its buildings. One of them – or what he took to be one of them – raised a cry of alarm. Soon he could see a collection of them, every one identical, spilling out of the buildings. They had not seen this kind of thing before.

Faced with such a crowd, he might have turned away or at least stopped, but he kept moving forward. One of the monks was studying the horse. This man said something to his companions, gestured that they should stay where they were, and struck out alone.

The horse had met the monk three times before. He could remember it now: meeting the weathered figure as he had climbed up to inspect the light on the horizon, then sitting together as they had watched over the carcass of another dead horse; then, most recently, he had met his quiet eyes out on the plain.

*

The horse had very little memory of how he had made it from the track into the small stable attached to one of the outbuildings of the monastery. Neither did he know how long he had stayed there. He knew that he had spent a long time, at first disintegrated in a heap on the floor, breathing uneasily and wracked by the affliction. Some of the time there were people about him, attending to his body, apparently nursing his wounds; at other times, he was left to rest and recover. When they came to him, he could see their looks of horror. They shook their heads; their brows furrowed, and they shared their disquiet in short exchanges of words.

The monk he had met before visited every day. He kneeled to feed the horse an apple, stroke its nose, and survey the horse's condition. The two of them would have talked had they had the words to make it possible. The horse knew when the monk was about to pet him, feed him or if he wanted to inspect or examine his injuries. Their eyes met frequently. Often the horse would wonder what thoughts passed through the monk's mind. What was the nature of the connection between them? How had they come to know and understand each other? Then came more questions: how and why had the monk come to be in the buildings where he had been sold into labour? Had the monk intended that he should find his way back to the mountains? And was it just a coincidence that the dim recollection of his origins in these hills had come to him at the same time?

Here in the valley, wrapped in the drifts of land, he also saw the monk in a different way; by outward appearance he was the same, but the horse could remember thinking when he had seen him on the plain that his appearance was a suggestive shadow. Perhaps because he could now remember all the details of the valley, the monastery and the hills, the monk no longer appeared in this light; the horse thought he could see the real person under the cowl.

When, eventually, he recovered enough strength to move about, the monks brought him out of the building. They treated him in a way he had never been treated before. All the humans to whom he had been bound had, in one way or another, saddled, tied or shackled him – they used equipment to control his movements and behaviour. In the case of the knight, this had felt natural and he had not resented it. In the case of the mill owner, it had felt unnatural and oppressive. Among these monks, they just opened the door to the stable and let him out. They attached nothing to him, and when he looked about him, he could see that there were no fences or walls to constrain him. If he had wanted, he could have bolted or galloped off in any direction he liked.

The men were scattered about in a disorderly throng. When they saw him emerge from the stable, a few of them clapped, then they smiled and cheered. He wandered about the grounds, as the men followed. A few of them broke off in a huddle of conversation. The stable opened onto a large, cobbled yard that gave way to a verge of grass. A low wall bounded the grass, but he could see a gap at one end that appeared to lead through to the very large and ornate building at the centre of the site. He walked haphazardly towards the grass.

Over the wall and across the fields, he could see the ridge of the valley. That was his home and, ultimately, where he belonged. The ridge rose steeply, but not so steeply that it couldn't be climbed. In fact, he thought he could see a line cutting diagonally across the hillside that had the appearance of a path, leading up to the ridge. Was it that easy?

He caught one of the monks moving through the gap in the wall. The figure followed a path that hugged the large building and led out through another patch of grass to a fence demarcating the complex of buildings from the surrounding fields. By now he recognised his distinctive features, but he could also sense the purpose behind the man's advance towards the fence.

The horse lowered his head, sniffing around

the ground, then looked back at the other habited men, standing around in conversation and quiet pleasure at the horse's recovery. Then, at a leisurely amble, he walked through the gap in the wall and followed the way that had been paved for him.

The monk whose lead he followed had reached the fence and was hunched over it, his head pushed back on his neck to look up at the ridge. Beyond, the horse could see another lonely figure at work in the field. Except the spectacle of the horse mingling with the community had halted his work. The horse kept his head low as he walked, sensing his way forward.

In motion, his body felt natural and familiar, but it did not have the unreflective ease of his usual movements. He ached almost everywhere, and his scars reminded him that he was not what it had once been. This little walk felt not unlike his return to the hills; it was something he knew instinctively but the knowledge of it had been obscured by his recent misadventures. He wanted the full command of his limbs in the same way he wanted to be where he belonged.

The horse reached the man propped up against the fence. He walked up to the fence so that the two were standing next to each other, and then nestled the man with his nose. The man hooked his arm under the horse's head, so that their heads rested on each other. The figure in the field continued to stare, and the other robed figures broke up their conversations.

Man and horse stayed in this embrace for a little while, until a bell rang out from the large building nearby. The bell, though he had heard it before, was much closer and louder, which startled the horse. The man comforted him and put him at his ease, but the horse could see that the man's companions were moving as a group. The bell was a signal. The monk held the horse in his gaze momentarily. Then he turned to join the rest of the group as they filed into the building.

The horse stayed where he was, standing almost completely still, expecting or waiting for something to happen. The valley was silent, save for the sound of the birds, until noise broke the silence. The horse raised his head, wondering what it was and from where it was coming. Then he knew. It was the men in their building; they were singing. He recognised the sounds. When he had heard it before, it had been more distant, an echo harmonised with the natural rhythms of the land. Here, it was much clearer. It was the 'call' he had heard at the head of the valley – the mysterious tune that had brought him there in the first place.

The horse held his position, listening to the singing. It was a strange, solemn lyric. He would never know what they were singing, but he wanted to get closer to it, as if proximity might unlock its meaning. He walked a little way along the path by the building. The chorus of voices gave way, leaving just one that sang a few lines before the ensemble returned. This lone voice followed by the chorus became a pattern, and to his ear, sounded like a conversation: the single voice called to the others and, in their turn, they answered.

The horse lingered by the entrance to the building, reflecting on the voices within. Then he walked slowly back to the stable and stayed there until the singing stopped.

*

The horse's stay with the monks followed this pattern. He took shelter in the stable, where he was fed, groomed, and otherwise tended, but they left the stable door open for him to roam around the site as he pleased.

Throughout the day, the men were kept busy, not least by singing in a routine that spanned day and night. The night offices were often the most haunting. The horse would sometimes walk out in the open air to hear the chorus, look up at the ridge and study the whispering shapes that the tricks of the moon cast on the landscape.

It was at night, listening to the men's song and looking up at the ridge, that he felt his strongest urge to leave the community and make his final return. Nothing was stopping him. But he had not yet seized the moment. He knew that a time would come when he would leave, but he didn't know when, or how he would recognise it. He had, by now, witnessed different forms of life. All of them had placed demands on him and asked questions of him. But what question was this community asking? They didn't want him to fight, haul, labour or use his flesh for their own pleasure. What then? Was he just there to listen?

His inner guide to the strange workings of the men told him that they were preparing him for his eventual return. They were mending his body, helping each incision to heal, but readying him in a different way, setting at ease the lingering jitters left on him after his various ordeals on the plain. They were bringing him back into alignment with his home.

These thoughts also told him that he had, in spirit, already returned to the ridge. He was only waiting for its final recovery before his body would follow; and his recovery was almost complete. One of the brothers visited him at least once a day.

Then one evening, around dusk, the monk the horse had come to trust appeared in the doorway of the stable. He stood still, his shoulder leaning against the frame of the door. The horse could see that the man was not really looking at him; his eyes were cast upon the floor, as if in thought or deeper contemplation. As he levered his body off the doorframe, the man turned to look at the horse and he gave a little smile.

Something about this little look and the pensive moment that preceded it, took hold in the horse's imagination. It stayed with him all night.

In the early hours – the morning was not far off – the horse heard the community of men start to sing among the faint glow of the candles he could just make out against the windows of the large building. He still didn't know what they were singing. It was strange.

The horse looked up at the ridge, and guided by the music, he set out through the stable door, walked across the courtyard, found his way through the outer fence and tracked across the field. The singing grew fainter as he climbed. A line of trees divided the field from the lower parts of the hillside, but he managed to find a gap in the trees that led to the path he had seen. Trees overshadowed the path and the abrupt edges of rocks loomed in the dark. He heard creatures rummaging about.

The path was rocky, broken and uneven. It rose over a few sharp humps, until it emerged from the woodland onto a hillside strewn with bracken. From there, it climbed into a sheltered kink in the ridge that receded into shadow as moonlight spread over the valley floor.

His hooves dislodged rocks on the path beneath

him, and they found their way onto a grassy path that followed a final stretch across the common and onto the ridge. The air freshened and he could feel a gentle breeze against his coat. He tried his legs at a gallop and found that the strength he had once known, albeit tempered by years of use and injury, was still there. He slowed to a trot. Light was breaking around the shape of the mountains behind him.

*

'You are back,' said Sweetbriar.

'Yes,' replied the horse.

'We didn't think you would come back.'

Sweetbriar was not obviously changed, but on closer inspection, it was easy to see that she had aged. Since the horse had last seen her, she had given birth to foals, who had grown into horses. She looked more weathered, as if over-exposure to the elements had been her main burden. She would never say so, but he was sure that he looked older too.

'No?'

'We thought you would come to no good. You saw many things, I suppose.'

'Things and people.'

'We don't see so many people. Not up here.'

'No.'

'Some of us thought …'

'Yes?'

'Around the time you went missing we found a body. No-one would go near it. Not for a long time.'

'You thought it was me?'

'Yes, but we never knew. No-one else went missing.'

'I saw it too,' said the horse.

In his time away from the hills, he had forgotten everything, including the carcass of the horse, but it had been one of the first things that had come to mind when he had found the valley, and now that he thought about it, the horror of it stood out in his mind.

'It was a terrible thing,' he added.

'Is that why you went?'

The horse thought.

'I don't know – there were many things at that time. Many things came to my mind.'

'That light you saw. We all saw it too. But you were drawn to it.'

'I was curious about it.'

'What was it?'

'A fire.'

'A fire?'

'It was a battle.'

'You were tempted by a breach of the peace?'

Sweetbriar sounded aghast.

'I didn't know it, but yes. It called to me.'

'The fire called to you?'

'Yes, the fire.'

Sweetbriar considered what the horse had said.

'Why?' she asked.

'To make something of me.'

'And did it?'

'Yes. For a time.'

Sweetbriar had mellowed with age. Unlike the horse, she would never have left her place in the moors and nothing would tempt her to do so; but whereas her younger self had closed her mind to the horse's sense of adventure, a part of her now wanted to know more. That he had lived to tell the tale intrigued her, and in the time that followed, they fell into conversations like this one more often than they ever would have in the past.

She found him one time on the narrow ridge that bridged the expansive moorland and the gradual ascent to the highest peak.

'What's it like? On the plain, I mean.'

'There are many different things to see. I only saw some of them, I suppose.'

'What did you see?'

'Not far from here, there is what they call a farm. There, different animals – including horses – are put to work on the land. They are shackled to devices of tillage so that their owners might nurture the land. In some ways, it's quite clever.'

'Is that what you did?'

'No, but I witnessed it.'

'Then what did you do?'

'I rode with a knight. A knight is a man, but a special kind of man. He is noble and honourable. He is a warrior, a fighter. I was his horse and together we fought in many battles.'

'What became of your knight?'

'He was killed.'

'In a battle?'

'No.'

'How then?'

The horse paused.

'I suppose, in the end, he lost his way.'

Sweetbriar changed her tack.

'Is being a knight a good kind of life?'

The horse thought of all the cruelty he had witnessed, the razing of buildings and the many ways he had seen men disfigure and maim those around them. Cries of pain came to him, howls of rage, blood on the cobbled streets, and the time he had once seen a dismembered hand lying at the base of a wall.

'It's not something I really understand,' he said. 'But at the time, it was right.'

'The plain sounds like a strange place, then,' said Sweetbriar, before she wandered away.

In these and other conversations, the horse re-lived his experiences. He had not stopped to look back on them, until now, but under scrutiny, he turned them over in his mind. And he found that his thoughts never ended with the answers to Sweetbriar's questions; the questions she asked only opened the way to recollection of everything he had lived through. All of it came back to him, so that he might trace each memory.

First there had been life on the farm; he could still recall the excited curiosity he had felt as he had watched the work of the other horses from his paddock, and even the strange exhilaration that came to him when he was saddled by the farmer. Then came life with the marshal and his introduction to the young knight, the many hours they had spent riding together in sport and the warmth of the dead deer's blood around his haunches. The battles, the bodies, the ghost, and the fiery keep – his memories of them all swept him up.

'And what did you do once your knight had been killed?' asked Sweetbriar.

'I lost my way, too.'

'How do you mean?'

'I drifted. First there were some bandits. Then, when they could find no more use for me, I was sold into a different kind of servitude with a different kind of purpose, but one for which I could find no real liking.'

He told Sweetbriar about his time with the girl and the image she had created of him. He told her about the songs and revelry in which he had played a small part. He told her how it had all come to a sudden and unhappy end, how he had then become a workhorse, the value of his being weighed only by the strength he had left.

'In the time that followed, any purpose I had known with my knight vanished, or at least it faded until there was nothing left of it. And that, I believe, was when my memory of this place returned. That was when I ran with all my strength to these hills.'

The horse mulled over it all.

'It's strange to look back on these things. At the time I didn't think about them that much. The plain is a place of action and noise. There's little or no time to think. The things I have told you just happened.'

At the time he said these words to Sweetbriar, he didn't really know what he meant by them. But later that night, in the earliest hours of the morning, he found himself thinking about what they implied, which was his current state of reflection. He had wandered a little way further up the ridge. From there, he looked down on the plain.

What he had meant to say was that reflecting on his experiences belonged to the hills – literally, he could look down on them. Whereas on the plain he was immersed in one activity after another, caught up in the struggle of one group of characters then another. It was a place with no or little memory. Things looked different from the ridge. He could see everything that had happened, survey the details of each moment, know their shape, the hard grain of their life.

In this state, one episode in particular from his adventures on the plain came to mind. He thought of the young girl who had brought him into her band of minstrels, but most of all he thought of the image of him she had crafted. On first sight, it had startled him – something in it created a strange kind of echo. From his position in the hills, he thought he could see his former self as if through the crude markings of an image.

The horse looked out, trying to recall the spot in the distance that marked the place of the burning castle he had once stormed, and where he had lived.

Then he started to move in a slow shuffle. He lowered his head, and stepped forward, rising steadily again, letting his hooves lead the way.

A breeze blew over the hills. His legs carried him forward. Mostly, they took their time, but where the terrain became more challenging, or it was necessary to navigate an especially boggy patch or surmount an awkward cluster of rocks, they showed a burst of life. By this awkward act of ambulation, the horse drew closer to the highest point. The cold drew about him. His head swept the ground, drifting in the wind and lurching with the exceptional obstacles of the climb. His hooves pulled up the peaty mud, layering the bottom part of his legs.

Apart from the wind, all was silent. There were no other signs of life. With a moment of notable exertion, he would exhale and he could see his breath vanish into the moorland air.

How long it took him, he didn't know; he had finished with any thoughts about his short journey. In time he arrived at the wide, flat peak of the hill, and trekked his way across it. He stopped only at the escarpment. There, he waited, his head still set to the ground. In a moment, he looked up.

The shadow of a dark cloud made its way over the plain.